ZAPPED!

Joe turned to join Tom and Frank, then stopped in his tracks. Floating a couple of feet off the floor was a statue surrounded by four ten-foot-high black pillars. The statue was the exact image of Mina, the alien girl.

Staring at the figure, Joe realized he wasn't looking at a sculpture. Mina had been turned into a work of art!

Tom confirmed Joe's suspicion. "That halolike glow is the stasis field that protects her. She looks just like she did when her saucer crashed."

"How do we get her out?" Frank asked.

"I can penetrate the field like this—" Tom moved forward, his hand out to reach into the glowing field. But as he stepped between two of the black pillars, a hum filled the air. At the top of the ten-foot cylinders, a thin band of red light appeared, pulsing and brilliant.

Then four crimson energy beams lashed out, carving sizzling tracks across the floor right at the spot where Tom was standing.

Books in the Tom Swift® Series

Available from ARCHWAY Paperbacks

THE
ALIEN FACTOR

FRANKLIN W. DIXON

AN ARCHWAY PAPERBACK
Published by POCKET BOOKS
New York   London   Toronto   Sydney   Tokyo   Singapore

AN ARCHWAY PAPERBACK *ORIGINAL*

An Archway Paperback published by
POCKET BOOKS, a division of Simon & Schuster Inc.
1230 Avenue of the Americas, New York, NY 10020

Copyright © 1993 by Simon & Schuster Inc.

Produced by Byron Preiss Visual Publications, Inc.

ISBN: 0-671-79532-5

First Archway Paperback printing June 1993

10 9 8 7 . 6 5 4 3 2

THE HARDY BOYS, TOM SWIFT, AN ARCHWAY PAPERBACK and colophon are registered trademarks of Simon & Schuster Inc.

A HARDY BOYS AND TOM SWIFT ULTRA THRILLER is a trademark of Simon & Schuster Inc.

Cover art by Michael Herring

Printed in the U.S.A.

1

Bombs away!'' Tom Swift laughed as he looked up into the inky darkness of the California night. A brilliant streak of light flashed across the cloudless desert sky, suddenly exploding in a spectacular fireball.

Tom felt himself relaxing more than he had in months. He had been looking forward to tonight's sky show for a while, and he was not disappointed. The Perseid meteor shower came at the end of every summer. Hundreds of chunks of space rocks, left over from the formation of the solar system, descended into the earth's atmosphere. Friction with the air caused them to glow with heat.

Usually, the rocks burned away before they

reached the ground. Recently though, Tom had read about a falling meteorite blowing the engine out of a New Yorker's car. Tom grinned as another fireball burst in midair. Missed me! he thought.

More meteors streaked across the heavens. I can't believe this show, Tom thought. You get a night like this only once in decades. He sighed, aware of the empty space beside him on the blanket. It would have been perfect, if only Mandy Coster had been along. The clear, cool desert night, shooting stars, and Mandy— now there was a romantic combination.

Except that Mandy wasn't there. She'd called that afternoon to cancel their date with the desert sky. "We can make it another night, can't we? Brenda's leaving for Paris on Friday, and Wednesday is the only chance for all of us to get together. We're going shopping at the mall."

"I'd think she'd be saving her money to shop in Paris," Tom had said.

"What? And arrive there looking like a dweeb?" Mandy's logic missed Tom. And he missed Mandy.

He aimed his gaze at another streak in the sky, a low whir filling his ears as the lenses over his eyes automatically focused. I must look like I'm wearing joke glasses with two-inch thick lenses on the frames, he thought.

In fact, these were zoom lenses hooked up to a light-intensification system.

Wherever Tom turned his eyes, the lenses magnified and brightened the image. He'd tested them the evening before with a little meteor-watching, but the show had been nothing like tonight's.

"Mandy," he sighed, "you don't know what you're missing."

Tom's lenses locked on a new shooting star high above. Then Tom sat bolt upright, squinting in amazement. The meteor had changed course!

Shooting stars couldn't do that. Only a craft with a pilot could move that way.

Tom kept his eyes glued to the falling object. He hadn't imagined it—the gleaming pinpoint of light changed course again.

It's moving too fast to be a plane, he decided. And it seems to be heading this way.

As he stared, his lenses kept trying to focus. But the image stayed blurry, just growing larger with frightening speed. For a brief instant, he got the impression of a saucer shape. Then the whatever-it-was seemed to swoop at his eyes, blinding them with a glare of boosted light.

Throwing up one arm as a shield, Tom tore off the mag-intensifier glasses. His eyes were still dazzled, so he didn't see the aerial mystery when it passed overhead. He felt it though, deep in his bones, as a sonic boom rattled through him.

Then came a high-pitched whine that tore at his ears, followed by an enormous crash. Tom's vision came back just in time to be blinded again by an explosion of light. Whatever it is, he thought, it cracked up just beyond that ridge of hills.

Tom scooped up his blanket, tossed it into his van, and set off cross-country for the impact site.

A little-used fire road led to the crest of the largest hill. Tom hit the brakes so hard the van shuddered. Below him stretched a shallow valley. And on the valley floor lay a tilted, crumpled saucer shape.

From this distance, it looked like an abandoned Frisbee, maybe a silver pie plate, but Tom knew it was much, much bigger. Snatching up a flashlight from the glove compartment, he vaulted out of the van and went skidding down the slope.

The closer he came to the saucer-shaped craft, the larger he estimated its size. "This sucker has to be thirty feet in diameter, and at least twelve feet high in the middle," Tom whispered into an eerie silence. Even the local crickets had stopped their calls after the mysterious crash. "Whatever it is," Tom went on, "it's no model or remote drone."

His flashlight glinted off the saucer shape's silvery outer skin. There were no scorch marks from its searing ride through the atmosphere. In fact, the strange metallic material seemed to gleam with an eerie iridescence, reflecting all the colors of the rainbow.

The crash site was brighter than the top of the hill. A pulsing golden glow reflected off the desert sands. Tom realized the radiance came from a jagged tear near the bottom of the crumpled craft.

Clutching his flashlight tighter, Tom headed for the opening torn in the saucer shape's hull. He caught muted sounds, like the crackle of static electricity. The glow was stronger here, but what Tom saw almost made him turn back.

The outside of the ship was silvery metal, but a crack in that outer skin revealed something that seemed almost organic. Oozing from around the exposed edges of the hole was a pale green mass, rapidly turning gray, then black, from exposure to the air. Tom would have liked to believe it was padding or insulation—something like that. But he'd never seen insulation that dripped a yellow-green liquid—a liquid that seemed to clot like blood.

"Gross!" Tom whispered, but he crept

closer, avoiding the growing puddle of fluid. Part of the graying mass quivered like jelly. Here and there, Tom saw silver filaments—wires?—that ran through the bulk of strange material.

Peering through the ragged tear, Tom got a glimpse into the deeper interior of the saucer, the source of the golden glow. All thoughts of oozing jellies were forgotten.

Tom faced a cylindrical room, maybe eight feet wide and ten feet high at the top of its domed ceiling. The walls were of the same iridescent silvery metal as the outside. Sections of the walls glowed with starlike glints. Controls? Sensors? One thing was sure—this was no technology he'd ever encountered.

The center of the room held the biggest mystery, though. Floating a foot off the floor was a glowing shape—the source of the light that spilled onto the desert.

The object was a statue, carved from some golden-hued material Tom couldn't identify. He estimated the figure as five feet and a few inches high. It seemed to be a life-size human in a black harness. Or rather, Tom mentally corrected himself, a humanoid—almost human. The statue had the right number of arms and legs, very shapely and seemingly female. A slim torso led to a human-contoured head. Its face was heart-shaped, with high cheekbones, a delicate nose and lips—almost elfin. But the eyes were the figure's most alien feature. They were large and green, with no whites, and looked like glittering gemstones. The hair on the statue was long, a deeper shade of gold and more metallic.

Enthralled, Tom stepped forward and reached out to touch the figure.

As soon as his fingers penetrated the golden glow, the halo of light vanished. There was still a gentler radiance coming from the walls, which allowed him to see the statue dropping. Tom flung out his arms to catch it. What if it smashed against the floor?

But his breath caught in his throat at the first touch. The figure that fell into his outstretched arms wasn't metal, plastic, or any other material he knew about.

It seemed to be flesh.

It seemed to be breathing.

It wasn't an *it* anymore.

The golden girl shuddered for a second, drew a deep breath, then turned those brilliant gemlike eyes to him.

"Ah . . ." Tom managed to say. "Uh . . ."

Then came a sound he recognized—not from inside the hushed room, but from the world beyond the crack in the saucer's wall.

It was a distant *thwip-thwip-thwip*, the clatter of helicopter blades slicing the air.

The noise snapped Tom out of his unbelieving daze. Of course, he thought, I wouldn't be the only one to see this saucer come down. The government would be tracking it and sending people here to investigate.

The golden-skinned figure, so surprisingly light in his arms, heard the sound, too. Her gleaming eyes went to the tear in the wall, then back to Tom. She said no words, but her expression was pleading.

For a second Tom thought what it would be like to be found by government investigators and treated like a zoo animal or some kind of circus freak.

He came to an instant decision. He had to get this strange being out of there before the choppers arrived. With the girl still in his arms, Tom headed for the tear in the wall, when a sudden movement caught his eye.

Tom hadn't paid much attention to the box at the golden girl's feet. At first glance it was made of the same silvery metal as the rest of the ship, except for the complicated pattern of fine gold wires crisscrossing its top. He thought it might be a control panel or the housing for some machine.

But at Tom's movement, one side of the metal box suddenly glowed, as if a brilliant light had switched on within. Complex patterns in searing colors flashed across the face of the machine, incomprehensible and hard for Tom's eyes to follow. He paused in midstep, staring in fascination.

Some of the gold wiring on the metal box's top unbraided itself and stood straight up. From the blank sides, cables appeared. The box had suddenly sprouted four whiplike appendages, which it used as legs to follow Tom and the mystery girl.

It flowed smoothly across the canted floor until it reached the puddle of oozing greenish goo. Then the cube-shaped machine suddenly stopped, as if it were staring.

Outside, Tom heard the clatter of the helicopters growing louder. Soon they'd be in sight.

Still holding the golden girl in his arms, Tom spoke to the mobile machine. "If you're coming with us, let's go. *Now.*"

Together, the unlikely trio dashed into the night.

2

It was almost eleven-thirty when a phone rang in the East Coast city of Bayport.

"Hardy residence," Frank Hardy said into the receiver.

"This is Gray Opinion Polls," the man on the other end responded. "Could you answer some questions?"

Frank snapped to alertness. This was no invitation for a survey. It was a recognition code from a government intelligence contact, the Gray Man. Frank didn't know the guy's real name, but he represented a top secret agency called the Network.

The Gray Man had gotten Frank and his younger brother, Joe, out of some major trouble and *into* a lot of dangerous situations as well. The Hardys were used to that. Peril was part of the territory in crime-busting, whether it came from helping their detective father or from one of their own investigations. Frank wondered what the government wanted now.

"We've been hired by the Burger Master fast-food chain to do some market research. Do you eat at Burger Master, and if so, how many times a week?"

Frank played along. "Once or twice a week. Oddly enough, we were thinking of heading there in about half an hour for a late-night snack."

The Gray Man had set the place, and now Frank had set the time.

"And which of the two Burger Master locations do you prefer to use?" the Gray Man asked.

"The one out by the Bayport Mall," Frank said promptly. The mall was closed now, and the late-movie crowd should be clearing out. This would make a good, quiet place to meet. Frank hung up the phone and headed into the living room to get Joe.

Just the mention of a secret meeting propelled Joe off the couch and upstairs to get dressed. Minutes later the Hardys jumped into their van and made quick time through the quiet streets, arriving early at the meeting place.

The parking lot of the fast-food joint was nearly deserted as Frank pulled the Hardys' van into a space beneath a light pole.

"So what do you think?" Joe Hardy asked flippantly. "Will he turn up driving a gray Studebaker? Or disguised as a drive-in waitress?"

Instead, the Gray Man stepped from the shadows at the far end of the lot, wearing a rumpled gray suit. He looked like an insurance salesman or an accountant, but Frank had seen this man fight hand-to-hand with terrorists and assassins and come out on top.

Joe rolled down his window. "What's up that we need all this cloak-and-dagger stuff?" he asked.

The Gray Man slipped a manila envelope through the window. "Look in there."

Frank opened the envelope and pulled out a flimsy piece of paper with a grainy picture on it.

"That photo was wired from California right before I called you. Recognize the van?"

Squinting at the picture, Frank frowned. "I can barely make it out. How do you expect me to recognize it?"

"There's a second page in there," the Gray Man said. "Enhanced surveillance photo, blown up."

Frank separated the pages to find the second picture, which showed part of a California license plate. He could make out four numbers.

"The government has been burning up phone lines and computer time matching that plate and the owner. Turns out he's a guy named Tom Swift, Jr.—a science whiz kid." The Gray Man glanced at the Hardys. "You two know him, I believe."

"We've met," Frank admitted. "Our dad asked his father for some technical help on a bizarre fossil. It turned out to be a hoax."

Joe nodded. "Yeah, Tom was a nice guy. He even offered to show us southern California sometime when we weren't out on business."

"Good," the Gray Man said with a grim smile. "Then he won't be too surprised when you turn up." The smile dropped from his face. "I need to plant somebody out there, close to him. Someone he won't suspect might be checking him out."

Joe stared at the government man, startled. "Checking out Tom Swift? What for? From what I know of him, he's a real straight-arrow."

The agent's face twisted in a frown. "I don't know the whole story myself," he admitted. "But we're supposed to get somebody on him right away." He paused for a second. "I can make an educated guess as to why, though Now that we have a new world order, the government has been changing assignments for all the intelligence agencies. The Network's big priority is technology smuggling. This Swift kid has access to a lot of high-tech prototypes, including military stuff. Terrorists would pay top dollar for that."

"You think Tom Swift is selling pocket atomics to terrorists?" Frank's voice was full of disbelief. "Not the guy I met."

"Maybe you should get to know him better," the Gray Man said.

"Besides," Joe put in, "who are we to turn down a free trip to California? Maybe a week or two in the sun will kill off this creeping crud that's been bothering me."

For the last week, Joe had been fighting an attack of summer flu. In fact, he'd been dozing on the sofa when the call from the Gray Man had come.

"If you're still under the weather, maybe we shouldn't go," Frank said, reaching for any reason to turn down an assignment he didn't like.

"My pills from the doctor finished today," Joe informed him smugly. "We can leave tomorrow morning."

"Good," the Gray Man said. "I've got a cover story arranged, both for your folks and the people on the coast. You'll be asked to courier some packages to Los Angeles, with an indefinite stopover."

Joe grinned. "California, here we come!" he crowed. Then he began to cough.

Frank shook his head. "I've got a weird feeling about this."

At the same time, on the other side of the country, Tom Swift pulled his van over to the side of a mountain road. He'd been driving for nearly two hours, first to lose the converging copters, then to collect his thoughts.

A few seconds of attempted conversation had convinced him that his alien visitor spoke no English. He tried Spanish, some technical German, and even a few Japanese phrases he'd picked up. The golden-skinned girl just stared at him with unblinking emerald eyes, completely blank.

She had tried speaking to him in a language that was mainly clicks and pops, long on consonants and short on vowels. Tom didn't understand a word. He doubted if anyone on earth would.

"You apparently don't speak any earth language. I guess that means you didn't expect to land here." He paused as another thought came to mind. "That ship you were in was small—only thirty feet wide. That would fit inside the wingspan of an F-16."

He frowned. "In fact, that cabin in your saucer wasn't all that much bigger than the body of a fighter plane. Most of the space inside seemed to be filled with that greenish gray goop. The area where I found you was only eight feet in diameter. Not much living space for a long voyage, even if you *were* in some kind of suspended animation."

Tom looked at the gold-skinned girl, who stared at him, frowning in concentration.

"I can't see anyone taking that thing you were in for a long journey—it was no starship," Tom continued. "And if you were on a scout craft from a larger vessel, you should know our language. So what was that saucer? A space-going life raft?"

The girl responded, perhaps to his change of tone. She moved closer, her face going from its lost expression to a determined one.

"I'll bet that's it," Tom said. "You're lost in space."

The alien girl was face-to-face with him now, very near. For a human, Tom thought, that kind of closeness meant either romance or an angry confrontation. Neither concept seemed to work here.

A flash of disbelief went through him as the girl's long, shiny hair did something no human girl's could. The golden strands were moving, but no wind was blowing. The hair was moving by itself!

Each strand is acting like the wires on top of that boxy robot, Tom thought, fascinated. But instead of standing straight up, the golden strands from the head of the alien girl were moving around his face, weaving together. Tom was so busy taking in the details that it took him a moment to realize his head was being encircled, encased in a cocoon of fine metallic-feeling filaments.

Wait a second, Tom thought. Images of bugs enmeshed in spider silk began running through his mind. He went to pull back, raising his hands to fend off the strange assault and twisting his body in an effort to pull free.

But as the golden strands touched his face, an arc of electrical current flashed through his flesh, paralyzing him.

Then everything went black.

3

Pure animal panic tore at Tom's heart. Although he realized he wasn't unconscious, he thought he'd suddenly gone blind. His face was tingling as if a million little static electricity charges were going off on his skin. His scalp prickled as if his hair were standing on end. Then blurrily, like a badly focused film, images appeared out of the darkness—hundreds of them, too many of them.

Tom blinked, but that didn't clear the confusion in his vision. He seemed to be in a corridor of some sort. But the image was repeated over and over, as if he were facing a bank of hundreds of TV sets or watching the hallway through the reflecting prisms of a kaleidoscope.

Wait a second. Those aren't reflections, Tom realized. Each single image is from a slightly different viewpoint. Slowly Tom put it together. The alien girl's faceted emerald eyes were compound eyes, and each facet was a separate light receiver. Tom knew that the only earth creatures with eyes like that were insects. But inside the metallic cocoon of the girl's hair, Tom was seeing a scene the way she would see it.

Now that he understood, the scene seemed to clear, turning into one picture. Or maybe Tom's brain was recovering from the sensory overload of the strange images crashing into it.

Tom could hear a high, hooting twitter—some kind of alarm? Maybe. Certainly, he was moving down the corridor at high speed.

His hand—no, a slender, golden-skinned hand—reached out to slam into a panel glowing in a color that Tom had never seen before. He didn't get a chance to stop and look. The panel and the wall seemed to vanish, revealing a familiar object—the saucer-shaped craft that had crashed in the desert.

The viewpoint changed drastically as he seemed to launch himself toward an opening in the saucer. A loud voice reverberated in the air, shouting in the clipped, click-and-pop language that the girl had used. The port he'd used to enter the saucer closed and became solid wall. Then the viewpoint lurched so violently, Tom could almost feel the craft's deck shuddering under his feet.

And then the saucer's overhead dome became transparent. There was darkness up there, darkness spangled with stars. A shape came tumbling into sight. It was a saucerlike mother ship with three rodlike nacelles—engines?—and a huge gash torn in its skin. Two of the engine nacelles glowed with an unearthly radiance, and that uncanny glow was spreading across the vessel's skin.

Tom had no idea of the starship's size until he realized the tiny saucer shapes around it were escape craft bursting from its sides. They were like fleas leaping from a dog. That ship must be miles wide, he thought.

Abruptly the starship and the cloud of escape ships vanished in a blinding flash. Tom felt a sense of desolation—aloneness. Then he realized that feeling didn't originate in his own mind. Like the images he was seeing, the emotion that flooded him came from the girl.

She must have stared through that clear dome until the exploded mother ship had become just a dazzling cloud in the darkness of space. Tom saw her slender golden hands reach down to a collection of straps attached to a black box. He recognized it as the black harness the girl had been wearing when he'd found her.

She put it on, and then the view disappeared in a golden haze. Sure, Tom thought, this is the glowing aura I found around her when I entered the saucer.

As suddenly as they had begun, the stream of images ceased. Tom found himself surrounded by a different kind of gold. It was the shining web of the alien hair—if it *was* hair. From the electrical shock and tingles it had given him, Tom suspected it was some sort of antenna or lots of antennae.

Now the golden strands were parting, releasing him. The delicate features of the girl's almost human face were very close to him. In the faint beam from the van's overhead light, Tom could make out something he hadn't noticed before. The girl's golden skin was composed of tiny scales, like a lizard's or a snake's.

She may look human, Tom thought, but she definitely is not.

For a long moment, they stared at each other. Well, Tom thought, it's about time to start some communication. He tapped his chest. "Tom," he said.

"T'm," she repeated, almost running the two consonants together.

Raising a hand to her own chest, she said, "M'na."

21

"Don't think I can say that," Tom said. "How about Mina?"

"M"na," the girl said, trying not to make it so clipped. "T"m."

"It's a beginning," Tom said.

Then the van's cellular phone began to ring. Mina jumped, but Tom made calming motions as he picked up the receiver.

"Tom? It's Mandy," the voice on the other end of the line said. "Still stargazing? We finished our shopping safari. I thought maybe you and I could still get together."

Tom's eyes went to the dashboard clock. He was amazed to see how little time his mind voyage had taken. Then he glanced at Mina. Instinct told him he should keep the alien girl's existence a secret. "Uh, can't do that, Mandy. Got some stuff to take care of in the lab. Uh-huh. Sure. See you soon."

Slowly the realization of what he'd done began to hit Tom. His impulsive rescue would mean new troubles at every turn. "You'll need a place to stay," he said. "I've got an idea on that. In the mountains there's an old government observation station that Swift Enterprises took over as a lab. Nobody's using it now, so you can live there for the time being."

Mina stared at him in complete bafflement, and Tom realized he was babbling. He looked

carefully at the alien girl. She wore a tight-
fitting jumpsuit, almost the same color as her
skin. The outfit was a little flashy, but with
some makeup and earth clothes . . .

That could wait till tomorrow, Tom figured
as he started up the van again. First he'd have
to get Mina squared away in the lab and let
her know when he was coming back.

It took Tom about twenty minutes to find
the place. At least the cot and bedding in the
old lab were clean. With the help of a pad and
some sketches, Tom did his best to explain
the clock and when he'd come to see her in
the morning. He left Mina and her boxy robot,
and headed home.

Better make a note to myself, he thought.
Or tomorrow I might think this was just a
crazy dream.

Thursday morning was more like a night-
mare for Tom. He arrived back at the mountain lab a bit later than he'd intended. Halfway
there he'd realized that Mina would need supplies. So he stopped off to pick up some food,
only to confront a new problem. Could Mina
eat the same things that humans did? Tom finally wound up getting a variety of foods.

As he drove along the little-traveled road
through the scrub brush at the bottom of the
mountain, new questions hit him. How do we

test this stuff? How do we know it won't poison her? Tom still had no answers as he pulled up on the bare, rocky ridge that fronted the whitewashed concrete box that was the lab.

A flash of gold in the window told him that Mina was up and watching. She opened the door, and he carried his packages in. "Good morning," he said, smiling.

Mina smiled back, then held up his pad, pointing from the time he'd drawn on the clock face there to the clock on the wall.

"I know I'm late. I got you some things to eat." Tom set his purchases down on a lab bench, unwrapping each item and taking a nibble, hoping she would understand.

Mina did, coming over and flashing him a smile, showing slightly too sharp teeth as she pointed to her mouth.

"I don't know if this stuff is safe, though."

As Tom was speaking, the strange, boxy device that had followed them from the wrecked ship skittered over to the bench on its whippy tentacle legs.

The golden wiring on top of the box uncoiled, and several strands inserted themselves into the various items like probes. Then the front of the box flashed with an alien script. The thing is a robot, Tom realized. It must be giving Mina readouts of its analysis.

Fruit, cereal, bread, and juice passed the

tests. But Mina looked dubiously at the processed cheese and cold cuts that Tom had brought. Skim milk passed, but regular milk didn't. At least she would have enough for a breakfast. Mina ate hungrily, licking a drop of milk from the side of her lip with a tongue that was slightly longer than human normal. Finishing, she gave Tom a grateful look and spoke to him in her click-and-pop language again.

"This is going to take a lot of work," Tom said. "Well, I've taken on big projects before." He used the pad again to show that he was going for more supplies. She seemed to understand, borrowing his pencil to draw a picture of the lab with a head in the window.

"You'll wait for me here? Good." Tom went back to his van and set off for the Central Hills Mall.

He had spent the night trying to come up with a plan for Mina. As a golden-skinned alien, she was just too conspicuous, but if he could disguise her as a human girl . . .

During the course of the morning spent in a department store, Tom found out just how much he had to learn about human girls. In the makeup department, he discovered something called total coverage, not to mention cream toner. "Does the young lady have lav-

ender or green tones to her skin?'' the saleswoman asked.

"Uh, I don't think so," Tom said. How
could he answer that Mina's skin seemed to
be gold and scaly?

There was still more: foundations and blush-
ers, loose powder, bronzers to imitate a tan
and the difference between spring and summer
complexions. Tom left with an armload of tiny
bottles, tubes, and jars.

Picking sunglasses was easy—Tom just got
the largest pair he could find. They would do
a fine job of hiding those inhuman green compound eyes.

Next came clothing. Ten minutes of walking
around racks left him completely confused.
Was Mina a size five or a size seven? This
stuff was worse than quadratic equations.

Finally, a motherly-looking saleswoman came
over. "Having a problem?"

"Er—ah, yes," Tom admitted in relief. "I
have to buy—"

"A present for your girlfriend, right?" the
woman said.

Tom didn't clear up that misconception.
"But I don't know her size."

"Sports clothes might be easier," she suggested, leading him to counters of brightly col-
ored clothing. "These only come in small,
medium, and large."

Tom picked up some jungle green shorts and a matching T-shirt. "These are nice."

"And the size?"

"Small." Tom held up the shorts. "No, medium." He held up the same set in that size. "Uh, no, small." Then back again. "Maybe medium."

The kindly smile on the woman's face began to look a little strained.

Tom sighed, reaching for his wallet. "I'll take them both," he said, admitting defeat.

An hour later Tom was back home, riffling through the contents of his sister's closet.

Sandra Swift burst into the room. "What are you doing in there?" she demanded, her blue eyes narrowed in suspicion.

"Just looking." Tom's excuse sounded lame even to his own ears. "I was thinking . . . about how hard it is for girls to buy clothes."

"What?" Sandra pushed her long blond hair back out of her eyes.

"All those crazy sizes, the weird way they set things up." Tom glanced over at her. "What's the difference between petite sizes and junior ones?"

Sandra laughed. "If you're thinking of getting a present for Mandy, it's easier just to ask a friend what size she is. You could even ask me."

"Umhmm," Tom mumbled.

"Anyway, get your head out of my closet," Sandra told him. "You've got company out at the front gate. Two guys you invited to stop by if they were ever back in the area—Joe and Frank Hardy."

4

Joe Hardy lay blissfully on a blanket, catching some rays. This Laguna Pequeña beach is a nice place to spend a Saturday, he thought drowsily. He opened his eyes, which were shielded by dark sunglasses, just in time to catch a pretty red-haired girl run by in a wild print bathing suit. Yeah, Joe told himself. Nice scenery.

It had been two days since he and Frank had arrived on Tom Swift's doorstep, and things had gone perfectly. Tom had not only remembered them, he'd arranged for the Hardys to stay at his house. Joe couldn't have asked for a better setup. They were right on top of their subject. And under the dry California sunshine, most of Joe's flu seemed to have disappeared.

Another pretty girl stepped into Joe's line of sight. She had long chestnut brown hair and wore a tangerine bikini that complemented a very nice tan. Joe recognized her as Mandy Coster. Judging from what he'd seen in the last couple of days, she seemed to be Tom's girlfriend.

Mandy was walking with her cousin Dan, a guy with a quick grin and long hair. Joe had found him a little flaky, but nice enough. He'd even taken the Hardys surfing earlier that morning. Dan was showing off a good physique in a skimpy pair of black Speedos.

"Hey, don't get on Tom-Tom's case," Joe heard Dan Coster tell his cousin lightly. "Sometimes he's a busy guy."

"I know that." But Mandy's forehead wrinkled, and her voice was full of worry. "It's just that lately I feel as if he's brushing me off. I haven't had a chance to be alone with him since that night he went off into the desert."

She looked unhappily at her cousin. "Can he be *that* mad at me?" she asked in a small voice. "Just because I didn't go to watch falling stars with him?"

"It's not just you, Mandy," Dan Coster said. "Tom's been pretty much blowing off everybody lately. Look at those tourons from the East Coast who're visiting with him now. Who's been taking care of them?''

"Shhh. Not so loud," Mandy cautioned, nodding over to Joe. "Besides, they're not tourons. They seem like good guys."

The younger Hardy took that as his cue to fake a light snore. This conversation was getting interesting. In spite of Joe's acting, Dan Coster lowered his voice. "Yeah, they're okay. And we've sure had the chances to find out. They're supposed to be Tom-Tom's guests, but is he ever around? Noooooooo."

Dan actually sounded a little annoyed. "He keeps foisting them on his sister or Rick Cantwell. He's even had *me* baby-sitting them. I mean, these guys are fine and all, but why should we be entertaining them?"

"So what do you think Tom is up to? Why all this secrecy stuff?" Mandy said. Joe felt sorry for her—he could sense the pain of a broken heart in her voice. But he was getting more and more interested. Frank and he were there to discover anything out of the ordinary in Tom Swift's recent life. Now he definitely knew their host wasn't behaving like his usual self.

"Chill out, Mandy," Dan soothed. "He's just distracted. That's why he's acting goofier than usual. You know how every once in a while Tom turns into a real lab rat." Dan suddenly deepened his voice into a pretty good impersonation of Tom's. " 'Sorry, people, I'm busy right now inventing gorpoblorcho.' Until he finishes with his interstellar underwear or whatever, he's always out to lunch."

"I've seen Tom like that more than once," Mandy admitted.

"And I've warned him about these squidlike tendencies," Dan said in a kidding voice. "The next thing we know, he'll show up in geekoid glasses with tape over the nosepiece. I was hoping you would save him from that."

"Well I can't if he goes around treating me like I'm some kind of contagious disease." Mandy bit her lower lip. "Tom *has* been acting different lately. He's a lot more nervous."

"Hey, do you think maybe he's got the Bride of Frankenstein down in his lab?" Dan said with a laugh. "Don't get all spazzy about it. He'll come around, as long as you keep cool. And the best way to keep cool is to take a swim. Come on!"

As Dan dragged his cousin off to the water, Joe closed his eyes again, this time in thought. Tom had been a pleasant host, but he did seem to have his mind on something else. Frank found that suspicious, and after overhearing this conversation, Joe had to agree.

Both Hardys had also noticed that Tom

seemed to be disappearing a lot. Now other people were noticing, too, and not liking it. Was Tom busy at work on some earth-shattering invention? Or maybe—

Joe's train of thought was suddenly derailed as a splatter of cold water landed on his bare chest. His eyes flew open and he jerked upright, to find a grinning Sandra Swift standing over him.

Tom's sister looked like a comic book jungle goddess in a leopard print swimsuit that displayed a trim figure and an excellent tan. She also seemed to be shaking half the Pacific Ocean out of her shoulder-length blond hair and onto Joe.

"Up and at 'em, hotshot," she teased, shaking more water on him. "Your brother got us an invite to a volleyball game, if you can manage to get on your feet."

Joe made his voice sound like an old man's croak. "I might make it if I can lean on you."

He took off his sunglasses and grinned up into Sandra's gleaming blue eyes. Hanging out with her had been an unexpected bonus on this undercover assignment.

"So what's the story on Mandy Coster?" Joe asked, rising to his feet. "She was just over here complaining that Tom isn't paying attention to her."

"Yeah, where *is* Tom anyway?" Sandra

growled, looking up and down the beach. "He said he'd be here."

"About Mandy?" Joe prompted again.

"Typical guy stuff," Sandra complained, scooping up a towel to dry her hair. "One girl likes you, so you always pay attention to someone else."

"Hey, *I* wasn't going to hit on her," Joe protested, putting an arm around Sandra. "I've made my friends here."

"Maybe it would be just what Tom deserves if you *did* flirt with Mandy," Sandra turned in Joe's embrace, suddenly looking serious. "I think he's hooking up with another girl, behind Mandy's back. He was asking me about girls' clothes, like he was going to buy something—but not for Mandy. And the other night I caught him creeping home with a blond hair on his shoulder."

Sandra fluffed out her hair. "Speaking as a born loxie—"

"Loxie?" Joe repeated.

"Blond—like Goldilocks," she said.

"I think you're hanging out with Dan Coster too much," Joe told her. "I've never heard somebody use so much Coastspeak."

"Anyway, I know blond when I see it—and Mandy is no loxie." She frowned unhappily. "I don't know what I should do about it. Mandy is a friend of mine, and I don't like the way my brother is treating her. Why keep her on the line when he's fooling around with a secret squeeze? Sooner or later Mandy's going to realize he's not spending all his time in his lab—he's sneaking off to see another girl.''

"It's tough," Joe sympathized as they started for the volleyball game. He saw that Frank was already there, which was good, because Joe needed to talk with him.

There was another way to take the facts he'd just picked up from Mandy and Sandra. Tom's distraction, his nervousness, his sneaking around . . . these could all have another explanation, and not a romantic one.

Tom Swift could be sneaking off to secret meetings with a spy—a terrorist interested in making a high-tech killing!

5

Tom Swift stood by the parked cars, glancing from the bonfire on the beach to his wristwatch. His friend Rick Cantwell glared at him, his tanned, handsome face twisting in annoyance.

"Hey, man, this beach party is for your friends Frank and Joe. You're supposed to be the host of this Sunday evening hoedown, so you can't just duck out two minutes after showing." Rick ran a hand through his sandy hair. "Besides," he said, lowering his voice, "I think there's somebody else who'd like to see you."

Tom turned to find Mandy Coster almost running up to him out of the crowd by the fire. She was wearing a hot pink shirt tied at the waist and a pair of tight black jeans. Tom was a little surprised. She usually wore old sweatpants and a hooded zip-up sweatshirt to beach parties.

"You're going to freeze—" he began. But his words were cut off as Mandy threw her arms around Tom and gave him a big kiss. He drew back a little. What was going on with her?

"Some of the kids said you weren't going to show," Mandy rattled on in a high, nervous voice. "But I knew you'd have to come. I mean, Frank and Joe are your friends, aren't they?"

Tom nodded halfheartedly. He wouldn't exactly call Frank and Joe Hardy friends, not after they'd waltzed in on him in the middle of the most exciting project of his life. If only he could devote himself full-time to the problem of communicating with the alien girl! But no, he had to tiptoe around his family and friends plus two surprisingly nosy houseguests.

I guess I can't blame them, Tom told himself. After all, their father is a detective. But if they find out what's really going on . . .

He'd found himself shuddering lately whenever he passed the stands for the cheap tabloid newspapers. They always had weird headlines like "Ratboy Escapes Government

Lab.'' He could imagine the field day they'd have if Mina were discovered: "Boy Scientist Living with Girl Alien."

Tom had moved Orb, his spherical robot brain, out to the small mountain research center. But even with his best portable computer on the job, they still hadn't managed a breakthrough in communicating with Mina.

"Tom?'' Mandy's voice cut through his thoughts. "Have you heard even a word I've said?'' She had snuggled close to his side, taking his arm and wrapping it around her shoulders.

Now he realized she'd been guiding him away from the cars and the bonfire, into the deeper shadows. "There's a blanket and a picnic basket hidden up in the dunes,'' Mandy said. "I thought we could just sort of hang out together, alone. Maybe even catch a shooting star, if we're lucky.''

Her big brown eyes gazed up at him, almost pleading. "It's been a while since we got away, just the two of us.''

Any other time, this would have been perfect. But this wasn't any other time. Tom had problems to solve, major ones. He shouldn't even be taking time off for this dopey party, except he'd been trapped into it by Rick and Sandra.

"Hey, Mandy, that sounds great. But,'' he

said awkwardly, "I can't do it tonight." Tom
dug in his heels, resisting her pull away from
the firelight. "I'm only spending a couple of
minutes, since Rick twisted my arm. Then I'm
turning Frank and Joe over to Rick and Sandra, and heading back to the, uh, lab. I'm
sorry."

"Yeah, I'm sorry, too. Sorry I bothered to
care about you." Mandy shrugged off Tom's
arm and began stalking across the sand.

He could only stare after her. What was it
with girls, anyway? Communicating with Mina
was tough enough. Tom wondered if all fe-
males were actually alien life forms.

Someone was moving to intercept Mandy,
he saw. It was Sandra, who seemed to be giving him a dirty look. More weirdness. Then
Tom dismissed the thought. He'd hang for a
little while with the Hardys, then make his
getaway back to the lab.

Mandy's eyes were so blurred with unshed
tears that she didn't recognize Sandra Swift
at first. "Mandy," Sandra said. Then Tom's
sister grabbed her hand, and the tears flowed.

"I just don't get it," Mandy sobbed. "Why
is he treating me like . . . like a distraction?
If he acted angry at me, I could understand
that. But being ignored—why?"

"I think I know." Sandra's voice was

39

angry. She began to tell Mandy her theory about Tom's inattentiveness.

As she listened, Mandy's face went from misery to fury. "You think he's seeing someone else and just jerking me around?"

"I don't like to say it about my own brother," Sandra admitted. "But let's face it, he's not very good with human beings. Give him a computer or a weird science problem, and he's right at home. Maybe he just can't handle this situation."

"Well, he'll be sorry," Mandy said grimly. *"very* sorry."

This time when she stalked off, she had people to see and things to do.

Minutes later Mandy and Rick Cantwell were dancing by the bonfire. They were near Tom, who was talking with Frank Hardy while Joe danced with a pretty redheaded girl.

"I can't believe Tom would do a thing like that," Rick was saying for about the fiftieth time.

"Rick, his own sister said he was fooling around with someone else. He's only been pretending to go to the lab. Actually, he's been sneaking off. Sandra even found a blond hair on his shoulder."

"Not surprising, considering Tom has blond hair."

"I mean a *long* blond hair," Mandy said in

annoyance. She grabbed Rick's arm. "Look, he's cutting out already."

Sure enough, Tom was patting Frank on the back and waving goodbye to Joe. The Hardys waved back as Tom headed away from the bonfire, away from the beach and toward the road.

"Okay, he's leaving—and way too early," Rick agreed. "So what do you want me to do about it?"

"I want you to get your car so we can follow him," Mandy said crisply. "If he really is sneaking off to see some blond bimbo, I want to catch them at it." She bared her teeth in a smile that had nothing to do with laughter. "I intend to make Tom feel as bad as I do."

Rick stopped dancing, his face twisted in an unhappy frown. "I don't know . . ."

"No one knows," Sandra Swift said, popping out of the crowd from where she'd been watching and listening. "And there seems to be only one way to find out. You're the boy genius's friend, and I'm his sister. But even a genius can do something wrong. We've got to straighten him out."

"I guess it can't hurt to check," Rick said, surrendering. He and Mandy waited until Tom had gotten into his van. Then they ran for Rick's old Jaguar. The car started with a low rumble. "You're in luck," Rick said over the engine noise. "I just tuned her up today."

"With what?" Mandy wanted to know. "A spoon? We'll be lucky if he doesn't hear us following him."

"Hey, I'm the one doing *you* the favor. Don't knock the car."

Tom had pulled out now, heading his van for the road into the hills. Rick and Mandy took the same route, following closely. They never noticed the green rental car rolling along a few hundred yards behind them.

"Looks like your guess was right," Frank Hardy told his brother as he kept both cars in sight. "Sandra Swift must have told Mandy."

"Judging from the way Mandy was standing at the edge of the crowd and glaring at him, I figured that's what it had to be," Joe Hardy said. He half smiled, watching the procession ahead of them. "You know, we may be off beam here. Swift's not driving like a guy on the way to a secret meeting."

Frank chuckled. "Either he's innocent or he's the most arrogant guy in California. Swift isn't taking even the most elementary precautions against being tailed."

"Not to mention that his pal's Jaguar is almost riding up his muffler," Joe added. "I think a brass band would be less obvious."

They continued up into the hills, taking smaller and smaller back roads. Finally, they were jouncing along a gravel trail. Frank had turned off his headlights and was following the red taillights of the other cars.

He couldn't believe Rick Cantwell had left his lights on. They were like a rolling beacon, warning Swift that he was being followed.

But apparently, Tom Swift wasn't looking in his rearview mirror.

However, the amateur pursuers did let some space open up between cars when Tom turned onto a steep, rutted track that climbed up the side of a mountain.

Frank brought the rented car to a stop. "From here, we walk. Either Swift's reached the end of the line or he's come up with a way to ditch us so we can't follow."

He pulled off the road, and Joe opened his door. "Good idea. Besides, we could wind up dropping the transmission on one of the ruts up there."

They began a climb that left them puffing a bit. But the Hardys still managed to keep the two slow-moving cars in sight.

There was one more turnoff on the track, leading right to the mountaintop. The Hardys followed Tom's lights as his van made the turn. A moment or two later, Rick Cantwell's Jaguar veered onto the road, and Frank and Joe had reason to be glad they were on foot.

Rick and Mandy had gotten only a yard or so down the turnoff when the night was torn by the unearthly scream of a siren.

6

Joe Hardy dove for some scrub brush as the section of road ahead of him was suddenly lit by glaring floodlights. The siren continued to wail, covering the sound of the Hardys hitting the dirt. As he landed on the ground, Joe saw that caltrops—rakelike lines of steel teeth— had sprung three inches out of the ground around the Jaguar.

Now Rick Cantwell couldn't move his car forward or back. He and Mandy were trapped in the middle of a circle of lights and steel spikes.

Frank, the technical-minded Hardy, was peering at the side of the road. "I think Cantwell tripped an electric eye or maybe a laser security system.''

Joe grunted. "Whatever's going on at the top of that mountain, the boy inventor doesn't want uninvited guests." He glanced unhappily at Frank. "Would anybody go to those lengths just for a little privacy with his girlfriend? I don't think so.''

"Something's going on up there," Frank agreed. "The question is, how do we get up to see it? Swift must have the place wired up the wazoo.''

"At least he's got the road covered," Joe agreed.

The siren suddenly cut off, and a moment later a figure appeared, silhouetted against the uphill section of lights. "Sit tight and don't move," an amplified voice warned. Joe recognized Tom Swift, carrying what looked like the remote control for a VCR. But from the way Tom's finger hovered over some of the buttons, Joe hoped nobody was going to get erased.

When he saw who'd fallen into his trap, Tom froze in his tracks. "What are you guys"—he cut the overpowering amplification, finishing the question in his normal voice—"doing here?"

"That's what we were going to ask you!"

Mandy said angrily from her seat in the car. "What's going on around here?"

Tom floundered for a second before he came up with a reply. "I—uh—I've got some work to do here."

"You said you were going to your lab," Mandy snarled.

"We've got a lab up here," Tom answered a little too quickly.

"And just who is 'we'?" Mandy inquired acidly. "You and your new blond girlfriend?"

Tom had moved into the circle of lights. Now Joe saw his face go pale. "I've got no girlfriend up there—but I do have a major project under way."

"Then you won't mind letting us see it, right, Tom?" Even Rick Cantwell's voice was full of doubt as he sat behind the wheel.

Tom was silent for a full minute. "I'm at a very delicate stage right now," he finally said.

"So delicate your friends can't come and see what you're up to?" Rick had gone from doubtful to suspicious.

"What's wrong with you guys?" Tom was beginning to sound desperate.

"There's *nobody* up there?" Mandy pressed.

Again, as Joe listened, Tom hesitated just a second too long to be convincing. "I told you before," he said. "There's—there's no other human being in that lab besides me."

Mandy's voice was low and cold. "I don't believe you."

"Neither do I," Rick said.

"And I don't believe you two!" Tom finally burst out. He sounded honestly angry now, Joe thought. But then a good act usually does have a genuine seed of emotion in it. Tom was leaning over the hood of the Jaguar. "You come out here spying on me for no reason at all—"

"No, no reason," Mandy mocked him. "Just what your sister said about buying clothes for somebody—someone who's 'not a human being' but leaves long blond hairs on your shoulder. What am I supposed to believe—that you're keeping a sheepdog up there?"

"I don't care what you believe. If you can't trust me, well . . ."

Tom pressed a button on the remote control box in his hand. The row of rakelike spikes, angled to take out Rick's tires, sank into the ground.

They were the caltrops *behind* the Jaguar, Joe realized. The spikes guarding the way up to the top of the mountain remained in place.

"You can go," Tom Swift said coldly.

Rick and Mandy both stared in shock. "Tom," Rick finally said, "stop acting like a—"

"Just *go!*" Tom cut him off.

The floodlights went out, and Joe and Frank both scrambled through the sudden darkness for better cover. They didn't want to be illuminated by the Jaguar's lights as Rick Cantwell backed away from the automated trap.

Over the muted rumble of the Jaguar's badly tuned engine, Joe could hear Rick Cantwell. "Of all the stupid stunts—" Tom's best friend fumed.

Joe could also hear the muffled sobs coming from the passenger side where Mandy sat hunched over.

When the car had disappeared back down the mountainside, the Hardys stepped out of the darkness to meet in the middle of the now empty road.

"Now we definitely know that Swift's up to something," Frank said, peering up toward the shadowy top of the mountain. "And I'd say it was something dirty."

"Suppose we crash his party?" Joe said. "Maybe we'll catch him selling weapons he shouldn't be selling. Or meeting somebody he shouldn't be selling to. If we do, I get first crack. Just one punch to that smug face—"

"If we're going to bust in, we'll have to find another way to the top," Frank said. "Unless you want to get caught on 'Candid Laser.'"

They circled the base of the mountain, trying to find another way up. The going was rugged once they left the road, but Joe managed to find a rough footpath leading to the summit.

Frank grabbed Joe's arm and pointed to a small box set in a bush and another on the ground. Both had lenses aimed at varying angles across the path. "More security," he whispered. "Swift must have every route covered."

"Every *easy* route," Joe agreed. They'd reached the far side of the mountain, a rocky wall that seemed to rise almost sheer to the top. "See any boxes on that?"

"No, because only an idiot would consider scaling that," Frank said.

"An idiot—or a Hardy." Joe cupped his hands together to give Frank a boost up. "He'll never expect us. We'll be coming in from behind."

"Remind me what a good idea this is when we get stuck about halfway up," Frank grumbled. Still, he put his toe in the cupped hands and leapt up onto the cliff face. A moment later, Joe came scrambling up after him.

The rock was sandstone, eroded by wind and rain. Although it looked impressively steep and unclimbable, Joe found that lots of toeholds and fingerholds had been worn into it. Some of these irregularities were *too* eroded, as Joe discovered when he began putting his weight on a little shelf of brittle stone. The worn rock crumbled away under his foot, rattling down the cliff face.

Joe's hands slid out of their holds and he teetered for a long second, watching the mini-rockslide bounce its way downward. His loose foot scrabbled, his hands clawing desperately at the pitted brow of the cliff, until he managed to stabilize himself.

"You look like a spider with a hernia—arms and legs all over the place." Frank's hoarse voice undercut the coolness of his joke.

Joe just clung to the rock, panting. "Well, it beats falling all the way back to the bottom again," he finally said.

"You okay?" Frank asked.

"I'll be fine." Joe reached up to test a new handhold, then started climbing again. "But when we get to the top, I get *two* shots at Swift. One for his girlfriend, and one for trying to turn my hair gray."

Joe took it a little easier for the rest of the climb. Soon enough, he and Frank scaled a final rocky outcrop to find themselves kings of the mountain. Below them on a rocky ridge, a squat white concrete building gleamed in the starlight, the large satellite dish on its roof throwing a deep shadow across the open space.

"Delightful place," Frank said, looking at the peeling white paint.

"Not exactly what you'd call a love nest," Joe agreed. "But a perfect spot to arrange an arms-smuggling meet."

They slid down toward the lab building, Frank in the lead, scanning carefully for any security devices. "No spy eyes, trip wires, or alarms that I can see," he said. "I guess Swift thought the cliff was protection enough."

A large, dirt-spattered picture window threw a wide swath of light across the bare rock.

"Want to take a peek inside?" Frank asked after a quick look-over.

"Yeah, let's," his brother said.

Crouched low to blend with the shadows and avoiding the slash of light, they crept toward the building. They took opposite sides of the window, slowly rising from the corners to get a glimpse of the inside.

Looks like a pretty bare setup, Joe thought, quickly scanning the painted cinder block walls and the simple cot in one corner, neatly stacked with bedding. The bank of computers taking up most of the floor space was obviously a new addition, as was the huge screen set up against the far wall. A litter of half-disassembled high-tech gadgets was spread across the top of the computer consoles.

Tom Swift leaned over the centerpiece of

the makeshift lab, making an adjustment to a connection between some of the open circuit boards and what appeared to be a silver basketball that stood in the middle of the scientific wreckage. Joe's eyes traced wires and connections to a cube-shaped unit with a glowing front. It looked like a futuristic portable TV. Gold wire from the top of the box was braided around several different connections.

A young blond woman with a deep, golden tan knelt beside the box, then rose to join Tom Swift. The two of them worked over the ball, so close their heads were almost touching.

"A blond who knows science," Joe muttered. "Maybe Mandy Coster was right to be worried. This girl looks kind of cute in that little shorts and T-shirt outfit."

"But why is she wearing sunglasses in the middle of the night?" Frank wondered.

"Why don't we ask them?" Joe said abruptly. Before his brother could say anything, Joe rose to his feet, found a good-size rock, and flung it through the window.

The old glass shattered and fell with a satisfying crash. Joe leapt through the empty frame, followed by Frank. Together they confronted the two conspirators. Tom stood frozen, gazing in shock at the unexpected interruption. The blond girl, however, made a quick move, reaching for a thin box on top of one of the computers. If Joe didn't miss his guess, this was the same remote control that Tom had used to run the lab's security.

"Oh, no you don't!" Joe yelled, vaulting over the computers to grab for the remote. They both reached the black box at the same time and wrestled for it.

Joe grabbed the girl's arm and got the surprise of his life as she yanked it easily from his grip. He got an even worse shock as the petite young woman, maybe half his size, picked him up by the front of his shirt and hurled him across the room!

7

While Joe Hardy was still in midair, his brother launched himself at the blond girl. Frank wasn't fooling around—this terrorist was too dangerous to play with. And Tom Swift was beginning to move into the fight.

Frank aimed a flawless karate kick, a high, roundhouse attack. He was good and fast, but his opponent moved with superhuman quickness. One moment, his foot was flashing to catch her in the side of the head. The next moment, the blond's hand had seized his ankle, spinning him out of control. He barely grazed her cheek. Then Frank found himself airborne, flying toward the wall.

Joe had reached it just ahead of him. He

crashed spread-eagle into the cinder blocks, then sank bonelessly to the floor. Frank landed hard, too.

Neither Hardy was about to admit defeat. They wobbled to their feet, determined to go a second round. Instead, they staggered to a standstill, goggling.

Frank's attack hadn't hurt the blond, but his high kick had dislodged her sunglasses. Now Frank and Joe stood frozen in the glare of a pair of uncanny, nonhuman, faceted emerald eyes.

"What the—" Joe began.

"What's the idea of you two bursting in here!" Tom said at the same time. Then he saw that the alien girl's glasses were off. "Uh—are either of you hurt?"

"Just our pride," Frank said, unable to take his eyes off the girl. "Look, Swift. The government knows something bizarre is going on. They sent us in to check you out."

"Yeah," Joe said. "We came in expecting an illegal agent." He stared. "Instead, looks like we've found an illegal . . . alien?"

Not only had the strange girl lost her glasses, but some of her tan had disappeared. Makeup, Frank realized. Her true skin tone showed as a splash of gold high on one cheek.

"Well, the secret's out so you may as well know everything." Tom sighed. "Her name is

Mina. As far as I've been able to discover, her people come from a star system somewhere in the direction of Arcturus. She's the survivor of a starship wreck near the outer edges of our solar system. I don't know if this was her destination, but her lifeboat crashed near here, and I picked her up."

Tom shook his head. "I knew the government had to be checking out an unidentified ship violating our airspace. But you know what would happen if Mina fell into their hands. Either a media firestorm and freak show—"

"Or she'd be locked up somewhere and buried under top secret seals," Frank said, finishing Tom's thought. "I begin to see your problem, Swift."

"That's only part of it, Frank," Tom said. "I still haven't been able to communicate with Mina, except on a very basic level."

"T'm!" Mina suddenly called out, her gleaming green eyes still suspiciously on the Hardys.

"It's okay, Mina," Tom said. "Okay."

She repeated the word, making it sound more like a clicked "Uk'y."

"That's the best you've been able to do?" Frank asked in disbelief. "I thought you had something already invented for problems like this. What did Sandra call it, Joe? A psychotronic translator?''

Tom gave them a look. "You guys sure have been digging up a lot about me."

Joe shrugged. "Your sister has been very helpful."

"Forget that," Frank said. "Why doesn't your gizmo work?"

"My machine was built to work on humans," Tom explained with a shrug. "After all, who else was I going to build it for? The problem is that Mina's people, the T'wikt'l, don't have brains like ours. They make a bad combination with the translator."

He pointed to the silvery sphere connected by all the hardware with the boxlike unit. "If you know about my translator, Sandra must have told you about Orb."

"That's your portable superbrain," Frank said. "The one you built the big robot to carry around."

"That is correct," a low, metallic voice responded from the silver ball. "Rob acts as my transport module."

"Rob—that's the seven-foot-tall steel dude?" Joe asked. "I was afraid we'd have to tangle with him here tonight." He glanced over at Mina. "Not that we didn't have trouble enough."

"Tom was trying to connect me to an alien

computing device that Mina rescued from her craft," Orb said. "We've been trying for the better part of this week. Unfortunately, we still have failed to communicate. Our systems are not compatible."

"Like when Frank swears at his computer?" Joe asked. "He's always complaining about different operating systems."

"This is a worse situation," Orb responded. "We're dealing with an entirely different technology."

"You mean these aliens are too advanced for us?" Frank said.

"Not really. It's a case of them—and their technology—being very different from what we're used to." Tom pointed to the guts of the various high-tech gizmos spread across the computers. "I've been trying to cobble together something to bridge that difference. Mina has been fascinated, but she hasn't been able to help. I've been sort of working in the dark."

He frowned. "So far, all I've come up with is a big fat zero."

Frank looked over the complicated, wired-together apparatus. "I can't even figure out what this stuff is supposed to do," he admitted. "But are you sure all these connections are okay?"

Tom leaned forward. "Like where?" he asked.

In moments, Frank had a swift-designed laser iron in his hands, and Tom was deploying the leads of a circuit tester.

"Usually, my brother zones out like this over a piece of techno junk with our friend Phil Cohen," Joe Hardy said to Mina. "Then I wind up talking to the girl involved in the case."

The alien castaway's gemlike green eyes stared at him in what to humans looked like complete bafflement. Joe sighed. "Of course the girl, whoever she is, usually understands me a lot better."

By the time Joe had run out of small talk, Frank and Tom had found several faulty connections.

"Guess this is what happens when I take on too much alone." Tom shook his head in annoyance. "Thanks, Frank. We're ready to try again. Maybe this time, we'll even get some results. Ready, Orb?"

"Ready, Tom," the round robot brain's quiet voice responded.

Tom signaled to Mina, who went to the square piece of alien equipment.

Tom pressed a couple of buttons. A low humming filled the air, and random static patterns filled the wall screen and the front facet of the alien robot.

Then the static turned into occasional blasts, interspersed with blurred, but recognizable, pictures. Alien scenes, weird vistas, flashes of starships, blips of inhuman script. These views flashed by almost too quickly for the eye to make out.

Too fast for a human eye, at least, Frank thought. Maybe not for a computer. He turned to look at Orb.

Beyond the round robot, Frank could see fewer of the static bursts on the screen.

"We have contact," Orb's quiet voice announced. "No wonder we had so many problems with compatibility, Tom. Although the interface is mechanical, the actual processing unit is organic."

"Organic?" Tom repeated.

"You mean there's something alive in there?" Joe burst out.

"Replicated neurons," Orb said.

"Brain cells," Frank translated for his brother.

"Fascinat—" Orb began, but the robot's voice trailed off in a loud, unmusical buzz. The screen filled with more recognizable images—human words and pictures.

Tom leapt to his pieced-together apparatus.

"Looks like the alien computer has taken over," he said.

Maybe this was a mistake, Frank thought. What do we know about this girl and her brain in a box? What happens how?

What happened was the last thing Frank expected.

Unconnected golden wires on the top of the box rose up. So did Mina's thick, flowing hair. It blazed out from her head for a long moment, looking like a golden halo.

The alien girl suddenly smiled, her emerald eyes turning to Joe, Frank, and finally, Tom.

"Yo," she said. "Maybe dis is beddah."

8

The three human boys stood silent. Tom instinctively glanced at the Hardys, their faces as wooden as victims of shell shock. He could understand why—he was just a step away, himself.

I'm surprised at how well Frank and Joe have been taking things, he thought. Maybe it's their detective background—the old "when you've eliminated the impossible, whatever is left, however improbable, must be the truth." Even so, like the Hardys beside him, he'd faced just too much strangeness in too short a time.

"Well, she's talking in English—sort of," Joe finally stated the obvious.

"Orb? You back on-line?" Tom asked.

"Yes, Tom," the round silver robot responded.

"Could you explain this—ah, interesting development? And the equally interesting accent?"

Orb was silent for a moment, although Tom knew the robot brain couldn't feel embarrassment. "I believe when the alien computer took control of the transfer, it accessed several language files Rob asked me to store in my memory. Rob was working on a program to reproduce the speech of a comedian who appears on MTV."

Tom sighed. "Which one?"

"Lloyd Oscar Lohmann," Orb replied.

"The Lord-awful Low-man!" Joe said. "I guess she does sound like him—except for the voice."

"We're lucky she can't sound *exactly* like him," Frank said dryly.

"So what're you saying?" Mina burst out. "I talk funny?"

"Let's put it this way," Tom suggested. "You're using a nonstandard dialect of our language."

The next word Mina used was definitely nonstandard. She seemed surprised at the boys' reactions. "Your program says to use that word when I'm a little annoyed."

"That word's for shock comedians," Frank admitted. "But it's not commonly used in social interactions."

"Orb, don't you have any other English-language programs?" Tom asked. "We've got to change this."

Mina shook her head. "Don't bother. It won't work. Now this program is set in my brain, I can't like, you know, just erase it." The way she spoke, it sounded like "dis program."

Joe stared. "You mean you're stuck talking that way?"

She shrugged. "Unless you got anudder language you want me to talk in."

Tom shook his head. "Well, Mina, now that you can pass as human and understand what's being said, I suggest you don't say much. In this part of the country, your accent sticks out."

"Okay, I'll button it. To tell the truth, I'll be glad to get out of this box and get a better look at your world. From what I've seen on the tube and gotten from Brother Box—"

"Brother Box?" Joe Hardy sounded confused.

Mina pointed to the cube-shaped robot, which got up on its cablelike legs and took a bow. In spite of themselves, Tom and the Hardys jumped backward. "I suppose you'd call him a computer," the alien girl explained.

"Orb suggested Brother Box had organic components," Tom said. "Is that true?"

"Sure," Mina said. "He's full of nerve cells, cloned from my brain. You could call him an extended memory for me."

"Your brain has an annex in a box that walks around." Frank Hardy was getting that shell-shocked look again.

"Yeah, and the sooner we get in touch with my people, the better." Mina knelt by Brother Box, whose front panel turned into a monitor screen. "According to our readings, you've got all kinds of gunk in your air. Poisonous stuff. Carbon monoxide, sulfur dioxide, all kinds of weird aldehydes . . ."

"That's just southern California atmosphere," Joe cracked. "They call it smog."

"Well, it's bad for Brother Box's brain cells and mine, too. If we're exposed too long, we'll wind up with damage. We could even wind up screwy." She looked at the boys. "I can't believe it's good for you guys, either."

"We've begun to stop air pollution," Tom said. "But it's difficult. Our major form of transportation—" His discussion of traffic required an explanation of cars, then of the internal combustion engine.

Mina's face showed disbelief. "You use

carbon-based fossil fuels? And engines that burn the stuff so imperfectly that they fill your air with poison? This is your main form of energy? What about fusion?''

"We've got a start, but it's not developed yet," Tom admitted.

"So you use all these dirty, toxic sources." Mina shook her head. "You guys got a lot to learn."

"Well, maybe you can help us," Frank said.

Mina's face became guarded. "We'll start with hyperradio, a faster-than-light communicator," she said.

Over the next five days, Joe Hardy began to feel more and more like a fifth wheel on a tour bus. Sure, he was in on Mina's secret. But Tom Swift was the one she talked to about this faster-than-light radio. They worked to translate Mina's alien knowledge into earth technology.

Frank at least understood some of what was going on and could contribute his expertise in electronics. Joe could tune a car with the best of them, but dirty, poison-spewing fossil engines were not what they needed. Sometimes he was used as a guide when Mina went out, explaining earth sights and quaint human customs.

Even there, Tom and Frank kept leaping in to be of service. The four of them tended to stick together outside, because of the cool reaction from most of Tom's friends.

Mina had not been a hit on the Central Hills social scene when Tom introduced her around. Rick Cantwell ignored them, and Mandy was frankly hostile. Sandra let Tom and Joe know she wasn't pleased at the way her friend had been treated. Even easygoing Dan Coster sided with his cousin.

Joe stood at the entrance to an electronics store at the Central Hills mall, lost in the Friday evening crowd. Inside, Frank, Tom, and Mina were prospecting for additional circuitry supplies. Joe sighed, feeling left out. Then, as Mandy Coster came up beside him, he felt caught in the middle.

"What do they see in that Brooklynese bimbo?" she demanded in fury.

"Well, she's different," Joe said, trying to keep things neutral.

"Yeah, that's the word for her," Mandy growled. "No normal person wears big black sunglasses like those indoors. Does she think she's too cool to live or something? When I think that she's the one Tom was seeing behind my back . . . just look at that hair! You know it can't be real."

You don't know the half of it, Joe thought.

Inside the store, he watched Frank rush over with some component he'd found. Tom and Mina clustered around, talking animatedly.

"I don't know where your brother fits in all this," Mandy went on. "At first, I thought he was making a play for this Mina, too. I thought it would serve Tom right. But look! It's as though she has both of them wrapped around her little finger." She looked worriedly at Joe. "I don't like it."

Joe had to admit to himself that he wasn't all that thrilled, either. Before he could say anything, the trio inside headed for the front checkout counter. Mandy stalked away.

But the bad feeling stayed with Joe. What did they really know about this alien? In spite of the way Tom warned them that Mina wasn't human, it seemed as if those words just hadn't sunk into the science-boys' heads.

It's as if the two of them really want to hook up with her, Joe thought, lagging behind as the others walked through the mall. Frank had her left arm, Tom held her right. Joe wasn't sure, but it seemed as if there was something more going on than scientific interest.

Okay, she's cute, Joe admitted to himself, with a glance at Mina's slim figure. She looked even better now that she was able to go out and shop for her own clothes. But if he, the partying Hardy, wasn't going after her, why were Frank and Tom?

It's as if, despite all the brains they've got, they just don't see any dangers here, Joe thought. They're so hyped over what they can learn, they're ignoring one big fact. She's an *alien*. We really don't know anything about her except what she's told us.

He'd listened as both his brother and Tom had tried to ask Mina about what things were like "out there." In Joe's opinion, her answers had been pretty cagey. Apparently, there was a loose governmental confederation setup covering a variety of races on lots of planets. But Mina never really revealed much about this confederation, nor how it worked. That made Joe wonder just how benevolent those alien rulers might be.

Joe ground his teeth in frustration. He and Frank had been out here on the West Coast for over a week now, supposedly checking out Tom Swift. They hadn't made any report. Not only had they hidden the existence of Mina, but for the last few days, Tom and Frank had been working their brains out so she could "phone home" to her people. They'd even been getting in competition with each other.

They're so distracted, Joe thought, doing everything she wants. . . .

Like puzzle pieces coming together, his concerned thoughts suddenly snapped into a horrifying theory: We really don't know anything about her. They're so distracted, they don't see any dangers here.

It was like something from a bad science-fiction movie. But what if Mina had some power that was *making* Tom and Frank act this way?

Then why doesn't this power affect me? Joe asked himself. Maybe I'm not around her enough. Maybe she needs people who are more simpatico.

Joe sighed. Maybe his theory was all wrong.

But if he wasn't wrong . . . if he wasn't being paranoid, Tom and Frank could be putting the entire planet in terrible danger. This is something bigger than three guys can handle, Joe thought, even if one of them is an ultragenius.

"Hey, Joe," Frank called over his shoulder. "What are you doing back there? Come on, catch up."

While Joe had been wrestling with his thoughts, a wider and wider gap had opened between him and the three ahead.

"You guys go on," Joe told them. "I'll catch you later."

He turned away from the main gallery of the mall, heading down a side corridor that ended in a bank of pay phones. Concern outweighed guilt as Joe fed a handful of change into the slot, then dialed 202—the area code for Washington, D.C.

No more fooling around, he told himself. I'll have to be careful about how I put it, so the Gray Man won't think I've gone crazy. Joe sighed. But he's got to know what's going on out here. I may be the only one who can stop an alien invasion.

9

The next evening seemed to go on forever for Joe Hardy. The Gray Man had told him the previous day that something would happen by the following night. Joe fervently wished the government man had been able to tell him exactly when—and what. Joe still hadn't decided what to tell his brother, Frank.

At first, it had looked as though the four of them wouldn't be leaving the Little House on the Mountain. That's what Joe was calling the research station where Mina was staying. The place was darker and even less pleasant after they'd nailed plywood over the window Joe had smashed. But Tom was confident they wouldn't be there much longer.

After a full day of work, Tom, Frank, and Mina were still in the makeshift lab Tom had slapped together—and behind his formidable security system. Then came the breakthrough. "If this configuration pans out, we'll have a working trans-light communicator in days," Tom announced.

"I think that calls for a celebration," Joe said. "How about burgers?"

His voice died out as he saw the look on Mina's face. "No burgers," she said. "But I could handle some pasta."

They wound up at a pizza place on the outskirts of town. After they'd slid into a booth at the front of the restaurant, Joe noticed Dan Coster, Rick Cantwell, and several other kids he'd met around town. A girl came out of the group, heading for the food counter.

"Here comes trouble," Frank muttered. It was Mandy Coster. She froze for a moment as she recognized the people in their booth, then glared at Mina, who was sitting beside Tom.

Tom's shoulders went up, and his head went down. Joe jumped to his feet as Mandy started for them. He managed to intercept her in the aisle, a couple of yards away from the table. "I'm going to kill her," Mandy said in a tight voice.

This is all we need, Joe thought. If she gets

her hands on Mina, the glasses will come off, the makeup will be smeared, and the whole story will come out. Either that, or Mina will give herself away by throwing Mandy across the room.

"You can't do it." Joe frantically searched his mind for a reason to stop the furious girl. "Look, Mandy," he whispered, "Frank and I aren't out here by accident. We're on a case, and Tom's helping us. If you make a scene, you're going to blow everything for us."

Every muscle in Mandy's body was tense, and her hands were clenched. "I don't believe you," she growled.

"Fine. Go ahead, make an idiot of yourself, and blow our cover while you're at it."

Mandy's angry gaze wavered. "You're telling me the truth?"

"I know you've heard that we're investigators," Joe said, mixing a little fact into what he was saying. "All I can tell you is that we're on government business."

Mandy's eyes went back to Mina. "And her?"

Time for a little more truth, of a kind. "She's the reason we're here."

Those words got him a scowl from Mandy that turned into a doubtful look. "Okay, I'll back off. But I'm going to check with

Tom. And if it turns out you're handing me a line . . ."

Leaving her threat unsaid, Mandy went back to the group of kids in the rear of the pizza place. A few minutes later she and Dan left, much to Joe's relief.

"What did you tell her?" Tom asked in amazement.

"Tell you later," Joe said. He knew he'd have to tell him, unless he wanted Mandy Coster out for his blood.

They still had their celebration, but it fell a little flat after the scene with Mandy.

Mina leaned against the tall seat of the booth, her shoulders slumping. "Look, guys," she said, "not to complain or anything, but I'm feeling kind of wiped."

"You and the rest of us," Tom admitted.

"Want us to see you home?" Frank asked.

"You got it, champ," Mina said with a weary smile.

Joe felt his muscles tighten in anticipation as they drove up the mountain road back to the research station. He'd told the Gray Man about this isolated location. If the government people were going to do anything, this had to be the place.

Tom stopped his van at the turnoff, fishing out the remote control for the security system. He pressed a button on the box, and they drove past the vehicle trap that had caught Rick and Mandy.

Then, about ten feet farther up the path, a beam of light suddenly stabbed out of the darkness. It caught Tom full in the face, and he brought the van to a screeching halt.

After a second, Joe's dazzled eyes could see more clearly. The gleam came from a heavy-duty spotlight flash, mounted below the barrel of an Armalite assault rifle. It was the sort of rig that some deer hunters used. In this case, though, a carload of kids was caught blinking in the glare. And the "hunting rifle," Joe knew, could spit enough lead in a second and a half to empty its twenty-shot magazine.

"Okay, Swift, lose that remote control," an amplified voice ordered. "Nice and slow—fingertips only."

Joe realized that the voice didn't come from the man behind the light. He glanced out the side windows of the van to see that they were now surrounded. Bulky manlike shapes seemed to solidify out of the shadows. The bulkiness probably came from bulletproof vests, Joe thought. They're all pointing assault rifles at us, too.

Slowly, carefully, Tom did as the unseen voice commanded. Holding the remote box almost daintily, he stretched his arm out the window and tossed the control away.

Tom had no choice, Joe realized, not with a gun pointed at his head. He had wondered how the Network would move on them, worried that Mina might launch a counterattack. She couldn't do that now, sitting in the van's passenger seat. They were trapped, like goldfish in a bowl.

"Now," the voice said, "out of the van."

Tom and Mina emerged slowly from the doors. Frank opened the rear door, and he and Joe came out, making sure their hands were visible. The four of them found themselves the targets of a good half-dozen assault rifles. Even Mina was careful to make no sudden moves. She'd seen enough cop shows and action movies on the portable TV Tom had brought to the lab. The alien girl knew what those guns could do.

Three agents converged on Mina, yanking her arms behind her back and slapping handcuffs on her wrists. Mina responded with a blistering string of words that Orb's program must have listed for use when *very* annoyed.

As they hustled her off to a waiting black car, one of the agents laughed. "Y'know, I was expectin' some foreign agent," he said in a thick Brooklyn accent. "But she comes from Bensonhoist."

Go on thinking that—till her sunglasses come off, Joe thought.

The shock had finally worn off Frank. He turned a grim glance on Joe, obviously figuring out what had happened. But he didn't say anything, even when the handcuffed Mina was hustled into the rear of a dark car with a government seal on the door.

Tom and the Hardys weren't handcuffed but led at gunpoint up to a truck parked behind the research station.

Joe brought up the rear. He had to smile as he was prodded in the back by an Armalite muzzle. They're putting on a pretty good act, he thought. With luck our cover won't be blown with Swift—as long as Frank keeps his mouth shut.

The gun barrel hit him again, harder.

"Hey, take it easy," Joe whispered. "I'm the one who called Mr. Gray."

"Who?" The guard pushed him onward.

"Mr. Gray." Joe used the Gray Man's Network code name.

The guard gave him a blank look. "Don't know any Gray on this team."

"Come on. You can't be in the Network and not know—"

"Network?" The man's voice was thick with scorn. "Your mistake, kid. We're Espionage Resources."

A chill colder than the gun muzzle at his back ran up Joe's spine. U.S. Espionage Resources was another government intelligence agency—a fierce rival of the Network. He and Frank had tangled with some U.S.E.R. agents before. Espionage Resources had been handling—or rather, mishandling—an airplane hijacking in which Frank's girlfriend, Callie Shaw, had been taken hostage. The Hardys had saved the planeload of people and shown up the U.S.E.R. agents, with some help from the Gray Man. The boys had also exposed a U.S.E.R. operative in San Francisco who had gone free-lance, selling high-tech secrets to foreign powers—very much like the case Frank and I are on now, Joe thought.

But he had worse problems to consider. No way would Mr. Gray, a Network agent, call in these people. Something had gone terribly wrong.

They reached the truck. Leaning against the rear bumper, a man was lighting a big cigar. In the circle of the lighter's flame, Joe saw gleaming black hair pulled back from a handsome face with a devil-may-care expression. A pair of glinting blue eyes took them in.

"Are you in charge here?" Tom rapped out furiously. "I demand to know by what right—"

"You're in no position to make demands, because you've *got* no rights," the man said, puffing his cigar. "You've just been caught in the middle of an illegal conspiracy. But because I'm a nice guy, I might let you in on a few things. Name's Jack Cates, by the way. I run this group of . . . technicians."

"For U.S. Espionage Resources," Joe put in.

The amused look on Jack Cates's face faded away. "You've got big ears, kid—big mouth, too."

Before Cates could say anything more, another of the armed guards came up. Joe noticed a portable radio strapped to the man's back. "Team Alpha called in. They've delivered the package to the patron. She's been transferred to another car, and the team is on the way back."

"Patron? That doesn't sound like a government code name," Frank said.

Worse and worse, Joe thought.

"Maybe because this isn't a government job," Cates said. He turned to the radio man. "Tell the team to meet us at the safe house. We'll be done here soon." Cates then turned back to Frank. "See, this is a private job—grab the girl, deliver her, and eliminate all witnesses."

"Eliminate?" Tom echoed.

An unpleasant smile twisted Jack Cates's handsome features. "Yeah. As in kill."

They were suddenly illuminated by a pair of headlights. One of the U.S.E.R. agents drove up in Tom's van and parked it in front of the truck.

"Hop aboard, boys," Cates said.

"Somehow, I don't think he means for us to drive away," Joe said in a numb voice.

"To be frank, I was thinking more of an auto accident," Cates admitted.

"That's why we weren't handcuffed," Frank said. "No telltale marks on our bodies."

"Bright boy. Now get in the van." Cates whipped a pistol from under his open flak jacket. "I mean, if you want marks, I *can* give them to you." He worked the action on the automatic. "They might find bullet holes, but really, wouldn't that be kind of an empty victory for you?"

Given that choice, Joe, Frank, and Tom got into the van. Cates stood by the driver's side window, his pistol aimed at Tom's temple. "Turn the ignition key, and shift into neutral," the government man ordered. "But if you hit the gas, I'm going to ruin the upholstery with your brains."

Behind them, the engine of the heavy truck rumbled to life. It rolled forward, ramming into the rear of the van. They lurched forward, up the incline to the top of the mountain.

Just days before, the Hardys had crept down that rocky expanse after climbing the cliffside.

Now they were teetering on the edge, ready to go down the hard way!

10

The van teetered sickeningly, seeming to hesitate before it finally went over the cliffside. Frank Hardy bit back a gasp. Joe considered trying out a few of the words from Mina's salty vocabulary.

Then they were plunging downward, with nothing between them and sure death a hundred feet below.

Tom Swift flipped up a panel on the dashboard and hit some buttons. "Hold tight!" he yelled.

"What do you—*whuff!*" Joe's words were cut off as a combination of airbags and weblike stretch cords suddenly deployed themselves all around the van's seats. In a split second, Tom and the Hardys were cocooned within a protective wrapping. "Something I whipped up for jet crashes," Tom explained, his voice muffled by the inflated bag in his face.

And just in time, he thought. The van wasn't just plummeting, it was tumbling end over end as it dropped. Tom gulped, pressing his face into the inflated restraint in front of him. Maybe a predeployed barf bag would have been a good idea, too.

He didn't see what interrupted their free fall—probably a rock outcrop on the cliff face—but he felt the jolt as the van smashed into it, then bounced off into space. It was like taking a kick from a giant. Tom and the Hardys were slung around in their cocoons, jarred but uninjured. The van pitched and yawed, going into a sideways roll as it hurtled down. The passengers were buffeted by the force of incredible gyrations.

If it weren't so deadly, this would—*ooooch*—be like a carnival ride, Tom thought. He closed his eyes, but that didn't help calm him down as the van lurched in all sorts of interesting directions. Maybe I should try to patent this effect and sell it to an amusement park—a real sadistic one.

Then they hit bottom.

Tom was flung into the smothering confines

of the safety bag with brutal force. The cords holding him in place cut into his shoulders and waist hard enough to leave bruises. He snapped back, and the van tumbled to a stop.

Worming a hand against the pressure of the airbags, Tom reached a button on his seat. He pressed it, and the van filled with a hissing sound as the bags deflated.

Frank and Joe Hardy were slumped in their webbing.

They didn't know what to expect, Tom thought. The impact must have knocked them half senseless. He slapped a wobbly hand against the webbing release mechanism at his chest. The safety network fell away, and Tom crawled up the crazily tilted cab of the van toward Frank.

"Snap out of it, guys," he muttered. "We can't hang around here."

Frank gave a low groan, forcing his head up.

"I think I'm going to blow dinner," Joe said in a strangled voice.

"The release is on your chest," Tom told them. "Come on! Move it!"

The Hardys managed to drop free, rolling on the floor. Frank tottered up. "Fire!" he said. "Got to get out."

"It's okay." Tom was trying to work a wedged door open. "The gas tank is surrounded with an inert foam. Our problem is the guys upstairs. They'll want a fire. If they don't see one, they'll probably start one."

They tumbled out, to find one of Cates's men silhouetted in the lights of the truck above. The man was leaning over the clifftop, a short green tube on his shoulder.

"Run!" Tom yelled.

Frank and Joe needed no urging. They both recognized the antitank rocket the man was aiming. When that round hit the gas tank, it would explode, no matter what.

Yells from above were quickly drowned out by a deep *whoosh!*—the sound of the rocket launching. None of the boys was watching. They were busy leaving the van behind as fast as their legs could carry them.

From behind them, the hilly desert terrain suddenly lit up as bright as day. A dull roar filled the air, and the boys were propelled forward by the shock waves as Tom's van exploded.

Joe gave a wild yell as he went tumbling, to be picked up by Frank.

Tom turned back to help. His prized van had disappeared, roiling flames rising from the spot where it had stood. A thick, oily mass of smoke rose like a mushroom cloud in the inky darkness.

"One good thing," Tom panted. "The guys up there can't see us now."

As they hurried along, the ground tilted downward again, leading to a dry stream bed. Tom skidded down the rocky wall and set off along the sandy bottom. "We'll cut cross-country, avoiding any roads," he said.

"To go where?" Frank asked.

"Where we'll be safe," Tom replied.

Not too long after, they were staggering down the hillside overlooking Swift Enterprises. "Looks like a 'musement park," Joe Hardy said.

Tom had never thought of it that way, but he saw what Joe meant. The science complex his father had created sprawled over several square miles, from the rocket launchpads and airstrip to the testing fields to the Swift family home built on the mountainside across from them. Although it was the middle of the night, he could see all sorts of activity still going on. Office and lab buildings were lit, still full of people, and in one corner of the complex, floodlights illuminated the huge dome of the fusion reactor. To Tom, this represented home—and safety.

Joe must have agreed. "Geddown there, call Wash'n'don," he said blurrily.

Frank reacted sharply to the way his brother was slurring words. "Hey, Joe, you all right? I can hear you breathing from over here."

Joe seemed to be gulping for air, his breathing harsh. Then he began coughing. Frank put a hand to his brother's forehead. "You're burning up!" he said, worried.

"We'll be able to take care of him once we get down," Tom said. He took the lead, picking his way down a faint path.

They arrived at the gate to the complex, to find Harlan Ames, head of security, standing at the guard post.

This makes things easier, Tom thought.

"Harlan," he said, "we need to button this place up. I'm expecting some trouble—people trying to get in here. Don't let them. And my friend Joe needs medical care—"

He stopped in some surprise. Harlan was fanning a hand in front of his face. "Blasted bugs," he complained.

Tom stared. There were *no* bugs around here. Swift Enterprises was protected by a battery of ultrasound generators, developed by Tom and his father.

Unless Harlan didn't mean flying, biting bugs, but electronic ones. Tom glanced beyond the security chief and spotted a large black car in the parking lot—a car with a government seal on the door. The last time he'd seen that sedan, it had been rolling off with Mina in the backseat.

There were figures in the car, black, bulky shadows—U.S.E.R. agents. Tom whipped around, grabbing Frank and Joe by the arms.

"Stop!" Harlan called after them in a voice that was obviously phony to Tom. "Stop or I'll shoot!" He did, too—a bullet that went high over their heads as they ran up the road.

Behind them, Tom heard a car engine starting up. The Espionage Resources people were coming in pursuit. Then a pair of headlights speared out of the darkness ahead, illuminating the fugitives.

Great, Tom thought. I should have expected another car on the road, ready to box us in.

But it wasn't a government-issue big black car up ahead. It was a familiar shape, a somewhat battered old Jaguar—Rick Cantwell's car. The person behind the wheel was familiar, too—Mandy Coster.

She screeched to a stop beside them and rolled down her window. "Tom," she said, "I tried calling, but Sandra said you weren't back yet. So I borrowed Rick's car, hoping to catch you. We've got to talk."

"Right now, we've got to get out of here, or those guys will catch us," Frank cut in, bundling Joe into the front seat. He and Tom dove into the back.

Mandy's eyes went wide as she saw the big black car roaring toward the gate. She whipped the Jag into a tight U-turn, fleeing up the hillside.

Tom looked back. The black car had reached the vehicle gate, which had not opened. It tore into reinforced steel rods, slewing halfway around.

"I think you can ease off on the gas, Mandy," Tom said, clutching the back of her seat. "They didn't make it out of the exit."

"Tom, who were those guys?" Mandy asked, deeply shaken. "Why were they coming out of Swift Enterprises?"

"You wouldn't believe me if I told you," Tom said. He ached to let Mandy know the whole story, but how could he ask her to believe it?

"Those guys are rogue government agents," Frank suddenly spoke up. "My brother and I are on a case, and I think we've just hit a major complication."

"Y'think it's connected?" Joe asked from the front seat.

"We were sent in by a government agency to check a report of technology smuggling," Frank said, frowning. "But when the hammer came down, we got picked up by an entirely different agency, whose people tried to kill us.

Now, it could be interservice rivalry. Or maybe we're seeing a coverup."

"An' U.S.E.R. is dirty." Joe coughed.

"It has been before," Frank agreed. "Remember that agent in San Francisco who decided to go into business for himself?"

"Wazizname—Starkey. We helped our uncle Hugh nail him," Joe said.

Frank nodded, his frown deepening. "But this is worse. Judging from the response, we're talking about corruption at a higher level. A *much* higher level."

Mandy was listening wide-eyed as she drove through the hills. "What are we going to do?" she asked.

"I know what *you're* going to do," Tom said. "You're going to get out of the line of fire. About two miles ahead, there's an old rest stop. Drop us there, then forget you ever saw us."

"Tom, you're in trouble, and I want to help."

"You already have, a lot more than I expected—or deserved," Tom said.

Mandy gave a brief, bitter chuckle. "Maybe I was overreacting."

Tom sighed. "Only because I was acting like a jerk. I really do care about you, Mandy. That's why you've got to drop us off and get away. I don't want you getting hurt."

"Tom's right," Frank cut in. "And I hope we don't have any more arguments about it. This looks like the drop-off spot Tom's talking about."

Ahead of them was a deserted rest stop. The only illumination came from a pay phone by the road.

For a moment Mandy mutinously sped up. Tom put his hand on her shoulder. "This is the help we need. Don't worry, Mandy. I'll be in touch."

Slumping a little in her seat, Mandy pulled the car off the road. "Just don't get too interested in any more blonds, okay?"

Tom grinned. "Promise."

Frank and Joe exited the Jaguar, followed by Tom. He leaned in at the driver's side. "Take a nice, slow, roundabout route back to Rick's," he said, "and—mmmph!"

Mandy flung her arms around Tom, yanking him down for a kiss. "You'd better come back all right," she murmured. "Or I'll be twice as witchy as I was this week."

"Wouldn't want that," Tom said. He held her tight for a moment, then stepped away. "Now *go*."

"Quite a surprising girl," Frank said as they watched the Jag's taillights fade into the distance.

"Y'can say that again—" Joe's words were cut off by a coughing fit.

Tom looked worried. "Maybe we should have let Joe stay with Mandy."

"You'd just have turned them both into targets," Frank said unhappily. "I hope you have some sort of plan, though. You've just stranded us in the middle of nowhere."

"It has one thing we need." Tom stepped over to pick up the phone, slipped a coin into the slot, and began hitting buttons—seven, nine . . . twelve . . .

"Where's he calling?" Joe muttered as Tom continued punching in numbers. "The moon?"

"Let him finish. I've got the phone next," Frank said. "We need to place a call to Washington—and get to the Gray Man."

Tom had finished with his dialing. He waited for a moment, then said only two words: "Schedule Blindeye." Then he hung up.

"That's all?" Joe said.

"It's all we need," Tom replied. "Let's go."

"I need the phone," Frank said.

"Later," Tom told him. "That was a call to Swift Enterprises, where we've got superfast computers to trace calls—if those U.S.E.R. goons managed to twist enough arms."

Frank looked at the empty road. "So where are we going to go?"

Tom headed out into the shifting sands. "Follow me."

They set off cross-country, deeper into the hills. A couple of miles of scrabbling up dry hillsides, then scrambling down the other sides, had Frank panting and Joe reeling on his feet.

"Swift," Frank finally said, "we can't keep this pace. Not with Joe like this."

"We're almost there," Tom replied, pointing. Ahead of them rose a steep, clifflike mountainside. In the light of the moon, it looked familiar—especially when Frank saw the satellite dish half-hidden by the mountaintop.

"You brought us back to the research station," Frank said in disbelief. "What for?"

"It's the last place those agents will look for us," Tom said.

"Yeah, because only a real bozo would come waltzing back. We've got only a couple of hours of darkness left, at best. I thought you were taking us to a hiding place, not trying to prove how smart you are."

"There's something in there that we need," Tom said.

"Like what?"

"Orb."

Frank threw his arms out. "Now, why

didn't I think of that?" he said. "Here we are, stuck in the middle of the desert. Of course the one thing we need is a tin-plated basketball."

Tom had to bite back an angry retort. Look at things from Frank's side, he thought. The poor guy must be worried sick about Joe. "Believe me, Frank, I've got a plan," Tom finally said, doing his best to sound calm. "But to make it work, we need Orb."

"Well, you'll get it alone. Joe is almost out on his feet. I'm staying with him."

Tom nodded. That was only fair, he thought as he trudged onward. Tom skirted the wreck of his van at the foot of the cliff, finding another route to the top. He arrived at the crest overlooking the research station to find things much brighter than he'd have liked. The Espionage Resources agents had torn off the plywood covering the wrecked picture window.

"Oh, perfect," Tom muttered. Inside the squat building, three men were stripping the lab. They had already disconnected the wall screen and had moved it to the door. Several computers had also been shifted. Anxiously, Tom scanned the torn-up room.

He breathed a sigh of relief when he saw Orb lying on a metal box by the door. Apparently, the men had decided to tackle the heavier stuff first.

As the agents wrangled the screen out the front entrance, Tom sneaked down the rocky slope to the rear of the building. The glow of headlights around the corner told him that out there was a truck, which the men were loading. If they would only keep busy for a few more moments . . .

Tom stepped over the empty windowsill, ran across the room, and scooped up Orb.

He was almost back to the window when the door swung open behind him. One of the men had returned. For a second the agent just stared.

Then he said, "You!" and whipped out an automatic pistol.

11

I'm dead, Tom thought, staring at the muzzle of the agent's gun.

Suddenly his eye was caught by a movement off to the side, from the top of the box next to the gunman. Long golden filaments unwound themselves and began waving in the air. It was Brother Box!

A fat blue spark leapt from the gold wires on the top of the alien robot to the agent's pistol. The gun flew from the man's hand. He squawked once, then dropped to the floor, unconscious. Tom dashed for the window with Orb tucked under his arm. He was already descending the cliff face when he heard a scrabbling noise overhead. Tom looked up to see the boxy shape of Mina's robot following him. Wires waved on the robot's top surface.

"It wants to come with us," Orb translated.

"I guess it's the least I can do after you saved my butt," Tom said to the alien robot.

With some of Brother Box's cablelike legs winding themselves around rocks and others offered as climbing ropes, Tom's descent in the predawn glow went much faster than his climb. He reached the base of the cliff, then scrambled up the easier facing hillside. At the crest he found the Hardys waiting for him.

Frank had an awful expression on his face. "Joe's passed out. I don't think it's the bug so much as dehydration." His eyes searched the dry landscape surrounding them. "And where are we going to get water around here? Unless . . ."

He glanced at the nearly hidden roof of the research station. "What's the situation up there?"

"Three of Cates's commandos," Tom said. "What did he call them? Technicians? Hired killers is more like it."

He watched Frank's face set in hard lines. "We can't go back up there. In fact, we'd better disappear. Brother Box nailed one of them, but they're sure to start looking around."

"Where are we going to go?" Frank looked upward. "It's going to start getting light in a little while. Then it'll get hot. That's going to kill Joe."

"I know you're upset at my leading you here, Frank. But I have a plan, and I need Orb to make it work. Now, I know a spot where we can get some shelter. It's just a few miles away. If we can carry Joe there, I can get to work."

Brother Box wound up carrying Orb in two whiplike tentacles. Tom and Frank each wrapped one of Joe's arms over their shoulders and staggered off with him. They'd gone only a few miles when Tom announced that they'd reached their hideout.

"Here?" Frank peered at a shadowy crack in the bottom of a hillside.

"It's a cave," Tom said. "Not marked on any maps I know of. I explored this whole area when my family first came here. There's room for all of us inside, after scrunching through the entrance. It's cool and dark."

"Is there water?" Frank asked.

Tom had to shake his head. Then he started up the hillside. "We're going to take care of that now. Get Joe inside."

"And *how* are you going to take care of it?" Frank demanded. "Are you and Orb climbing up to pray for rain?"

Tom looked at him. "I know you're worried

about Joe. Just accept that what I'm doing will help him.''

Besides, he thought, you wouldn't believe me if I told you.

When Tom carried Orb back down half an hour later, he found Frank and Brother Box trying to make Joe as comfortable as possible on the rocky floor of the cave. He was conscious again and moving restlessly. "Thirsty," he croaked.

"What now?" the older Hardy asked.

"We wait," Tom told him.

"You know, Swift, this 'trust me' stuff is really beginning to get old."

"Another hour at the most," Tom said. Looking at Frank's face, he took pity on his friend. "The coding I did on the telephone was to get through to Rob, my other robot. Schedule Blindeye is a special command. It means he's to ignore all other commands, except the ones I give him."

"Well, I didn't hear you shouting up there," Frank said. "What were you doing, using mental telepathy?"

Tom held out the silver ball. "No. I was using Orb. They have a radio link, you know."

Less than forty minutes later, a larger-than-human figure appeared at the head of the valley leading to their hideout. It was Rob, Tom's giant robot assistant. His long legs got him to the cave in short order. His usually polished metal skin was dulled with dust, and he carried what seemed to be a collection of large plastic bags in his arms. He unwrapped the bags to reveal a wide assortment of items: camping supplies, a lantern, emergency rations, and several plastic gallon jugs of water.

Frank helped him unload, immediately taking the water to Joe. As he bathed his brother's face and gave him small sips, he glanced dubiously at the metal man. "Carrying that stuff cross-country, you must have stood out a mile. I hope you didn't lead anybody to us."

Rob put a metal hand to his chest. "I'm hurt," he said. "To think I risked getting sand in my gears taking the least-traveled routes to get here."

"I didn't notice any inconspicuous ways out of the Swift complex," Frank said.

"Well, there is one," Rob responded. "You know that pretty stream that cuts through the property? That's how I went out, underwater, following the stream bed. Easy enough, if you don't have to breathe. Then I just homed in on Orb's broadcast."

Rob swung down a large plastic bag he'd been carrying on his back. "In here I've got a change of clothes for each of you, money, and whatnot.''

"And no one at Swift Enterprises suspects?" Tom said.

"I wouldn't go that far," Rob admitted. "Your parents were asking me a lot of questions. I left a note for them, with the message you gave me through Orb. There is one other person who may have a glimmering, but he's definitely on our side."

"Who?" Tom demanded.

"Harlan Ames," Rob answered. "He's taken a lot of heat from the government guys swarming around the place for letting you get away. According to them, the Hardys are student terrorists who are using you, but Harlan has a hard time buying that story. I think he still wants to help you, using me as an information conduit. In my hearing, he dropped the fact that one of the mobile labs is in town for its annual motor vehicle inspection."

"A mobile lab, eh?" Tom looked thoughtful. "That would go a long way toward filling in for my van. It's not quite as well-equipped, but it would give us wheels and some tools."

"And I know where we should go," Frank suddenly spoke up. "San Francisco."

Tom turned in surprise. "I thought you wanted to get in touch with your friends in Washington."

"That was my first idea. But if these guys are trying to smear us as terrorists, I don't know if anyone in the government will still listen to us. We need to know more about U.S. Espionage Resources and what they're involved in. U.S.E.R. has a regional office in San Francisco. Whatever's going down here is being run from there."

"So those people will know what's going on with Mina." In the brief respite they'd had from running for their lives, Tom had been thinking and worrying about the alien girl. Where was she? What was happening to her? He turned to Rob. "Do you know the gas station where the mobile lab is being inspected?"

Rob gave them the address.

"We'll pick it up this evening, as soon as the place closes," Tom said. "A quick check for any bugs, and then we'll be on the way to Frisco."

The business district of San Francisco was quiet, especially on a Sunday night. The mobile lab was comfortable, but it was a long drive up from Central Hills, and the hour was late. The building Frank Hardy was staring at was a fairly low, solid-looking structure that had survived a couple of tremors and an actual earthquake not so long ago.

It housed the West Coast command center

of U.S. Espionage Resources, disguised as the offices of the Transmutual Indemnity Insurance Company. Hugh Hunt, a friend of the Hardys' father who worked in the shadowy world of espionage, had set up the cover years ago. Frank and Joe had discovered the truth during a case in San Francisco, where they'd wound up uncovering a U.S.E.R. agent's double-dealing.

Tonight Frank had the job of breaking in. He stood across the street from the ornate brick Transmutual building, in the doorway of another office block. Now he set off for the building next door to his target.

This was a slightly shabbier, smaller office building. He hadn't seen a trace of a janitor, much less a security guard. Frank reached into his pocket and brought out the small box Tom had handed him. It was one of Swift's high-tech toys, perhaps as long as his hand. A thin filament of optical fiber stuck out of one end. Frank inserted this into the lock, leaving it there until a barely audible beep came from the box. Then he removed the box from the lock. He could feel warmth through the palm of his hand, emanating from the inside of the little gadget. Then came another beep, and the box split open.

The interior showed a little plastic key, now cooling, surrounded by a "mold" of thousands of tiny wires. Tom had explained the principle. The optical fiber took a picture of the working end of the lock, which was encoded to the wires, making a mold for a small amount of melted plastic. When the key hardened, it would be almost as strong as metal and it would open the door in front of him.

Tom had demonstrated the machine by scanning the locks on the Swift Enterprises mobile lab, then creating keys to open the doors and work the ignition. They'd driven off in the van, picked up Joe, who was beginning to feel better, and headed up the Pacific Coast Highway for San Francisco.

Frank tapped the key. It had hardened. He slipped the plastic construction into the lock, and turned it. The door opened. Frank entered the building, then took the fire stairs up.

He emerged on a dark rooftop. All the neighboring buildings were taller than the one he'd broken into. U.S.E.R. occupied two floors of the adjoining building to his right. The first U.S.E.R. floor was just one story above this rooftop.

As he stepped out into the darkness, Frank reached into his pocket again, this time taking out what seemed to be a pair of bulky eyeglasses. Tiny motors whirred as he scanned the line of windows, operating the zoom lenses on the eyeglass frames. As Tom had promised, the lenses magnified what he saw tremendously, as well as boosting the available light.

The buildings were quite close, almost touching, and it would be no problem to climb to one of the windows on the U.S.E.R. floor.

Frank flicked a switch on the side of the lenses, and the scene changed, blurring slightly. Tom had added a new wrinkle to these magnifiers. Now they also worked in the infrared spectrum. Frank detected several hot spots on the glass window across from him—alarm sensors, no doubt, but they could be bypassed.

Digging his fingers and toes into cracks between the bricks, Frank began scaling the wall, aiming for a window in the middle of the building. He was just below it, and stuck his head up slightly to look in, when the window suddenly blazed with light.

The glare of light amplified through his goggles nearly knocked Frank from his fragile footholds. He clung as hard as he could, scrunching his eyelids shut and grabbing up with one hand to remove the apparatus.

Above him, the window opened and someone tossed a match out.

"Leave it open if you're going to smoke that thing," an irritated voice said from inside.

"If you insist," someone else, with a deeper, more casual voice responded. A moment later, a cloud of pungent cigar smoke wafted from the open window.

"Can't we get down to business?" the irritated nonsmoker demanded. "Why did you call us here at this time of night?"

"We need a council of war," the cigar smoker said. "Washington is getting a little testy. Our friends there were willing to go along with some political intrigue, even a little judicious secret-leaking to keep themselves in business. But they're nervous over the way this operation has gone. They think we're doing too much for our patron."

Frank kept very still. There was that word again.

"They're not the ones dealing with Mr. Sunshine," the first speaker said, the irritation only growing in his voice. "He's got a lot of leverage on us."

"Enough to get the colonel here to scoop up the wreckage of that experimental craft," the deep-voiced man agreed. "Even to check up on the people stealing Mr. Sunshine's technology. But I think you went a little far when you okayed getting rid of the witnesses, especially when one turned out to be Tom Swift. He's a little too prominent."

A new voice broke in, nervous and rushed. "Mr. Sunshine has enough on us to put us in prison—rock-solid proof that we've been leaking weapons technology to unfriendly nations and terrorist groups. We *had* to play along!"

"Besides," the irritated man added, "the other two—the Hardys—were too connected. We couldn't leave them around to talk. They had to be eliminated."

"But they weren't eliminated," the deep-voiced smoker said grimly. "Your boy Cates just messed up a van, from which the occupants miraculously escaped. Now Swift's father is raising the roof, wanting to press charges and know where his son is. Our colleagues from the Network are horning in, too. They want to know what proof we have that the Hardys weren't working in the national interest."

"Well, you two are the superspies," blurted the nervous voice—the colonel, Frank suspected. "Can't you manufacture some evidence?"

"It's much easier if the people we're smearing aren't around to contradict the 'evidence,' " the deep-voiced man said. "We can't ask you for any manpower, Colonel. But maybe you can ask Mr. Sunshine for some technical help."

"That's right," grumbled the irritable-voiced government agent. "We need some high-tech assistance to cover up for Mr. Sunshine, and he'll just have to provide it. I mean, we already delivered the girl who stole his whatever-it-was. He's probably taking her apart now, finding who she works for.''

Frank clung to the wall below the window. Whoever this Mr. Sunshine was, he didn't sound like a pleasant sort. Not when he had Mina in his hands—and might be taking her apart.

12

Frank decided he had heard enough. After quickly descending the wall of the Transmutual Building, he made for the rooftop entrance. In moments, he'd left the small office building and headed for the street corner where Tom and Joe were waiting in the mobile lab.

"I don't see any incriminating documents in your hands," Joe said as Frank climbed inside the lab.

"No, but I got an earful. There were three fairly important types in an office—two U.S.E.R. agents and an army colonel. They were discussing their problems, which included us being alive."

"Tell us more," Tom said.

"Apparently, these guys and some people in Washington were afraid the world might be getting too peaceful."

"Which would threaten their jobs," Joe said.

"Right. So they decided to leak some weapons information to unfriendly nations just to keep the pot boiling. Sound familiar, Joe?"

"It's the case we were sent out here to check." Joe looked at his brother, shaking his head. "I thought Mina was just a distraction, after Tom turned out to be a dead end. But where does Mina come into it?"

"That's the weird part," Frank admitted. "Remember how Cates said he wasn't working on a government mission and that he had a patron? Well, that person is apparently acting as the information conduit to the unfriendlies. His middleman position gives him a lot of leverage with the crooked U.S.E.R. bunch. They arranged for this 'Mr. Sunshine' to get hold of the wrecked saucer and Mina."

He shook his head, puzzled. "Here's a bit I don't understand. They seem to think Mina *stole* the saucer from him. But they also know what she is, because they mentioned him taking her apart."

Tom sat up very straight, staring at Frank.

"We've got to find Mina and save her!" Then he frowned. "What was that name?"

"They were calling the guy Mr. Sunshine," Frank said. "Do you know him?"

"I know of him," Tom said. "His name is Eric Laidlaw."

"Of Laidlaw Armaments?" Joe suddenly cut in.

"Exactly," Tom said, a little surprised.

"And how would I know?" Joe finished. "I read a little more than the sports pages, you know. When it comes to guns and the people who make them, I research. There was a good book on the Laidlaws—*Armsmakers, Kingmakers*. They've been at it almost a hundred years."

Tom nodded. "Since around the turn of the century, they've manipulated world politics, at first from Britain. The grandfather made a fortune in World War One and moved the company's operations to this country. What people don't realize is that the three generations of Laidlaws have made amazing contributions to technology."

"Weapons technology," Joe said.

"Yes, but their discoveries spurred other research, which had entirely new applications," Tom said. "The fact is, when it comes to patents, the Laidlaws as a family have more than almost anybody."

"Almost?" Joe asked.

"Except for the Swifts, if you count my grandfather Barton, my dad, and me."

"So what have we got?" Frank said. "A plot by the military-industrial complex . . ."

"Or at least a military industrialist," Joe quipped.

"Looks like this Mr. Sunshine is trying to keep up the family tradition of kingmaking." Frank frowned. "Of course, wars usually make for profits in the weapons business."

Tom looked even more grim. "I think this has gotten a lot more serious than mere technology smuggling. Laidlaw has gotten his hands on Mina and what's left of her ship. That gives him a lot of alien technology, including a possible space drive."

"Not the toys I'd give to an ambitious warmonger," Frank agreed. He looked at Tom and Joe. "Maybe the time has come to call our government contact, at least to tell him about the Laidlaw connection. Let's find ourselves a pay phone."

After punching in the 202 area code, Frank dialed the contact number for the Gray Man. Joe and Tom crowded in to overhear.

In spite of the late hour on the East Coast, the call was answered immediately.

"I thought it might be you," a sour voice on the other end of the line said when Frank identified himself. "Although from what I've been hearing lately, you've got a new employer."

"Things must have changed at the Network if you're so willing to believe what U.S.E.R. says about your agents, even irregular ones like us. Why did they suddenly wind up in charge of the raid on that lab?"

"Orders from higher up," the Gray Man said in a flat voice.

"It may be that some of those higher-ups are dirty." Frank quickly ran over the high points of the conversation he'd overheard at the U.S.E.R. office.

"They specifically mentioned people in Washington?" Frank noticed that the Gray Man's voice had thawed considerably.

"Apparently, they were concerned that the coverup wasn't working," Frank said. "Of course, if word got out about what they were doing with Mr. Sunshine . . ."

"Mr. Sunshine?" the government agent repeated. "The big arms merchant?"

"The very same," Frank told him.

"I've heard some whispers that he was involved as a pipeline for weapons technology. Not his own technology. Other people's weapons."

"No profit in giving away your own stuff," Frank said.

"Let's hear more about this meeting," the Gray Man said.

Frank obliged, relating it almost word for word.

"Well, U.S.E.R. does face a problem of redeployment," the government man said, almost to himself. "And that's something you wouldn't know. A Laidlaw connection might prove very interesting. You've given me a lot to look into. Until this gets straightened out, I can't pull you in."

"We sort of figured that. But we do need something."

"I'll help, if I can," the Gray Man said.

"I need modem links and the access codes for several government computers."

"Oh, I see. You don't need very much," the Network agent said snidely.

"Air defense, naval construction, army transport . . ."

"Just what are you looking for?" the Gray Man asked.

"There was an air crash in southern California about twelve days ago," Frank said. "We want to find out where the wreckage was taken."

"And this will help our case?"

Frank could have cut the doubt in the Gray Man's voice with a knife. "It might. This is what brought Tom Swift into the situation. It's also a link between Laidlaw and U.S.E.R. That bunch will now be trying to pin the technology leaks on him. And he's innocent.''

"What about this kidnapped girl?"

Tom shook his head vigorously. No way did he want Frank telling the whole story.

"She was an innocent bystander," Frank said, improvising quickly. "In the wrong place at the wrong time. So what about those government access codes?"

The Gray Man sighed. "Hold on."

Over the phone, Frank heard the quick rattle of computer keys being punched. "Got something to take this down?"

Tom reached into a pocket, whipping out a microcassette recorder.

"Shoot away," Frank said.

The Gray Man began reciting a string of letters and numbers, with the occasional password thrown in.

"Here's one you didn't think of," the government man added. "Army construction battalion." Another string of code followed.

"Enough for you?" the Gray Man asked.

"It gives us a place to start," Frank said. "How do we stay in touch?"

"Call in from time to time," the Gray Man said. "I guess that's the best we can do."

They hung up.

"What now?" Joe asked.

"I think we need a quieter place than a pay phone to try cracking those machines," Tom said.

They got back in the mobile lab and drove to the edge of town, returning to the motel room they'd taken on the way in.

Tom removed the portable computer from the rear of the van and took it to their room. Frank carried Orb.

Cobbling together a set of connections took a few minutes, but Tom soon had both computers attached to the phone system.

"I hope this doesn't run up our bill too much," Joe muttered.

Tom worked quickly and soon was hanging up. "Air Defense pinpointed the location where the saucer set down. I think I'm going to try for the records of that construction battalion." He glanced at Frank. "I mean, one of the conspirators *was* a colonel. Who else would he order in?"

The codes quickly got Tom in. Frank watched Tom's fingers dance across the keyboard. He works that thing even faster than I could, Frank realized.

Tom's face grew grave. "Yeah. The construction battalion was sent to the same map coordinates, moving the wreckage they found there to a San Diego location—a factory owned by Laidlaw Industries."

Frank nodded. "So the mysterious Mr. Sunshine definitely has Mina and her spacecraft. He must consider us a serious annoyance, while U.S.E.R. is embarrassed that we're still alive."

"And we know how Cates and his people handle embarrassments," Joe said grimly. "They eliminate them."

13

Tom fought down a feeling somewhere between amazement and annoyance. "I can't believe they just shipped that wreck off, like so much scrap metal."

Joe and Frank exchanged puzzled looks. "We're not following you," Frank said.

"These government people—U.S.E.R. and the colonel—they had an alien spaceship on their hands, and they just threw it away."

"Maybe they didn't realize what it was," Joe suggested.

"One look at this thing would be enough to start you thinking. It was a high-altitude aircraft with no wings." Tom shook his head. "The hull had a hole in it, and you could see the organic computer material. It was even bleeding. How could anyone ignore all that?"

Frank frowned. "Let's take it a step at a time. For one thing, the people who moved it didn't know how high it could fly."

Tom looked at him. "How—"

"Air Defense would have spotted the saucer's entry on radar. Maybe they got the helicopters out looking. But the construction battalion that did the moving would come from someplace completely different. They'd just be ordered to move some wreckage— high-tech stuff, but they couldn't tell how high it had been flying. If they wondered at all they'd probably think it was some kind of experimental hovercraft."

"And what about the brain tissue and the alien blood?" Tom wanted to know. "They'd have to think it came from another planet."

Now Joe spoke up. "Tom, you saw this thing come down. They didn't. You also saw a clincher that nobody else found at the crash site."

"What's that?"

"When you went into the flying saucer, there was an alien in it."

Tom had nothing to say to that. But Joe went on. "Before you saw Mina, did you even suspect that the bleeding stuff you saw was an organic computer? I thought you figured that out later.''

Thinking back to how he'd entered the alien ship, Tom had to admit they were right. "I wondered what it was, but I didn't have a clue,'' he finally said. "As for the greenish yellow blood, I was making sure I didn't get any on my shoes.''

"What would you have thought if you found the thing without an apparent pilot?'' Frank asked.

Tom twisted his lips in annoyance. "I'd probably have thought it was some kind of drone, running on remote control. But it still would have seemed weird.''

"It probably was weird for the guys in that battalion. I bet they were told to keep it secret. Knowing the army, and depending on how much pull that colonel I heard has, they may even have been shipped off someplace to keep them incommunicado.''

"I still think someone should have known better,'' Tom insisted.

"Who?'' Frank asked. "The conspirators leaking our technology through Laidlaw? For one thing, they'd just want the whole thing swept under the rug. For another, they wouldn't have the whole story. From the way I heard them speaking, they honestly believe the saucer was some sort of gizmo Laidlaw was experimenting with. That's what Laidlaw must have told them."

"I can see it now," Joe said. "Laidlaw calls the U.S.E.R. agents, letting them know he's lost something valuable, which has crash-landed near Central Hills. The agents contact the colonel to get the manpower to pick up the wreckage."

Frank nodded. "Meanwhile, the Espionage Resources people try to track down the pilot. Apparently, Laidlaw told them Mina was some sort of corporate spy. With you involved, they probably believed that story."

"Sure," Tom said in disgust. "Swift Enterprises has a *big* corporate spy network. We steal all our best ideas."

Joe continued. "But you have to remember, those agents must live by intrigue. It would make a convincing cover story for them."

"Plus there's the fact that they had to move fast—and they had a proverbial gun aimed at their heads. Laidlaw had a hold on them. He knew they were leaking secret information. If he let that fact get out, their careers would be over."

"I still think the government blew it," Tom said bitterly.

"It's not so hard to do," Joe consoled him. "The government's a pretty big entity, you know. One hand usually doesn't know what the other is doing."

"Besides the compartmentalization, you've got the usual petty politics, short-sighted though they may be," Frank added.

"Short-sighted?" Tom growled. "This is more like complete blindness. In return for hushing up some dirty business, those people gave away our ticket to the stars—not to mention stranding Mina here. And then they kidnap her. Of all the greedy, stupid—"

"Face it, Swift," Frank said. "Sometimes the government screws up on a massive scale."

"They didn't know what they had," Joe agreed. "But they did give it to someone to study."

"Yeah—Eric Laidlaw, merchant of death," Tom said bitterly. "His two interests in life are coming up with new ways to kill people and keeping the world destablilized so people will buy his weapons. He's just the guy to give a starship to. There are maybe three or four people on earth who would be worse."

The Black Dragon, for one, Tom thought. In his hands, that spaceship would have been a complete disaster. Or Yuri Takashima. He'd use it to turn space into his own private empire.

Still, Eric Laidlaw was bad enough. "Every

scientist on earth should have a crack at that alien ship," he said. "Universities, research groups—"

"Outfits like Swift Enterprises," Joe put in.

"Of course!" Tom replied. "We'd have a good shot at figuring out how the craft works, maybe even repairing it. If the world sees anything come out of Laidlaw Armaments from this discovery, it will probably be a better bomb."

"You really think that if the government knew what it had—an alien spaceship—it would have opened it up for every scientist in the world?" Frank asked.

Tom opened his mouth to say "yes." Then he closed it. That would have been the *last* thing the government would do. They'd have wrapped it in a cloak of secrecy. That had been the first thing that ran through Tom's mind when he saw the wreck.

The saucer would have been moved to a warehouse somewhere, and either forgotten or poked at by government types. Maybe in time word of its existence would have leaked out. Then Stanford would have gone to war against MIT over who would tinker with it next. Swift Enterprises would have been in there fighting, too, Tom had to admit to himself.

"Okay," Tom finally said. "You made your point."

"So Eric Laidlaw managed to cut through a whole lot of red tape with a little blackmail," Joe said flippantly. "I guess it pays to have friends in high places."

Frank nodded. "Somebody in air defense must have tipped him off about the saucer's entry into the atmosphere and the fact that it seemed to be controlled."

"What bothers me," Joe said, "is how he knew to go looking for a pilot. Those agents who nabbed us were there to get Mina first and get rid of us second."

Tom bit his lip, fighting the worry he felt over the alien girl. "What do you think they're doing to her?" he asked. "Frank, the people you overheard mentioned taking her apart."

Frank shook his head. "The more I think it over, the more I'm convinced they meant that in the sense of interrogation." He managed a smile. "We know that the U.S.E.R. guys who went off to deliver her never tumbled that Mina wasn't what she seemed—a human girl."

"From Brooklyn," Joe added with a chuckle. "I guess she didn't take her shades off to show those crazy eyes."

"Beyond that, all we know is that she's in Laidlaw's hands now. They're probably trying to find out from her how the saucer works."

Frank tried to keep things calm. "At least they can communicate."

Tom tried to tell himself that was a good thing. In other hands, Mina might have wound up on a dissection table somewhere. At least Laidlaw's people knew she was too valuable to harm. So far.

"Okay," Tom said, "we've got a better picture of what's going on. The next thing is to figure what we do now."

A roar of engines filled the motel parking lot. Joe glanced out the window, and his face went grim. "We say hello to trouble," he said. "I recognize some of Jack Cates's boys out there. Now that they've tracked us down, I'm sure they're eager to finish the job they botched before. Namely, eliminating the witnesses—us."

14

Tom and Frank leapt to join Joe at the window. The parking lot was filled with noise as six heavy-duty motorcycles swooped across the pavement, taking positions to cover their motel room door and the mobile lab. "Well, we're not leaving through the front door," Frank said grimly.

"First time I've ever been cornered by a bunch of rejects from a cheap science-fiction movie," Joe said.

"Oh, I'm afraid those cycles are for real," Frank said.

Joe had to agree. The roaring vehicles looked more like small tanks than road bikes. It was hard to see where the machines ended and the riders began. Streamlined cowling covered the fronts of the bikes and also wrapped around the riders' legs. The handlebars were built up, some with weapons mounted on them. One cycle even boasted a small rocket launcher.

Just the sort of thing some tinpot dictator would like to have surrounding his state limo when he goes out to look over the peasants, Joe thought. "Think they'll get some attention from the local police?" he asked.

"We chose this place because it was isolated and cheap," Frank said. "The front office has lots of pictures of cycle gangs who've passed through here. I doubt if anyone will pay much attention."

Tom had already moved to disengage Orb from the phone line. "Is there a back way out?" he asked. "I should have checked."

"I did already," Frank said. "There's only the bathroom window, and that's too small. We're trapped in here."

A moment later the door burst in, and Jack Cates stood in the open doorway. He held a large, beeping black box in his hand. On either side of the menacing agent, underlings aimed guns at the boys.

"Nice little gizmo," Cates said, smiling. "Led us right to you."

"Yeah, it only took you a couple of days," Joe needled.

"Wrong," Cates said, his expression turning ugly. "We were in the air as soon as you called Washington and were zeroing in while you were hacking into the computers."

A sick feeling settled in the pit of Joe's stomach. The Gray Man had turned them in!

"But we can discuss that later," Cates said, beckoning them out. "Come on."

"If you think we're riding piggyback on those bikes—" Joe began.

"No, you'll ride in my HQ," Cates said, marching them out. "As long as you're alive."

Joe realized that another vehicle had come into the lot, somewhere in size between a van and a mobile home. Now it pulled up beside the Swift Enterprises mobile lab. The superbikes were parked in a row behind it.

As one of Cates's technicians held the trailer door open, Joe, Frank, and Tom were herded inside at gunpoint.

The interior was like a cramped office, with a map table, computers, and sophisticated communications gear. Cates sank into a swivel chair that was fixed to the floor and gestured for his prisoners to take the three other seats in the place. He drew a pistol to cover them.

"O'Neill," Cates said to one of the guards, "you get behind the wheel up front so we'll be ready to leave. The rest of you make sure we're not disturbed.''

Smiling, Cates turned back to the captives. "That call to D.C. was a mistake. We knew you had a contact with the Network, so we bugged his line. When you called him, we traced back and found you were calling from San Francisco. So we scrambled some choppers where we were—''

"Laidlaw Armaments, down in San Diego,'' Joe cut in, annoyed at the government man's bragging. "I suppose they supplied you with all these new toys.''

Cates's intense blue eyes narrowed. "You're a good guesser,'' he said flatly. "It's just as well we're going to shut you up permanently. Besides, you're not as smart as you think you are. Hacking into all those government systems from one phone wasn't so bright. We knew where you were going to try from the access codes your contact gave you. All we had to do was tap in there, wait for your call, and trace it. If you'd moved around to do the job, you might have gotten away. But no, you just hung out here, like sitting ducks.''

His handsome features set in a sneer. "You may be bright enough, but you're amateurs.''

"Not like you and your people,'' Frank said.

The rogue agent nodded. "We were set up

for years in Cyprus, moving all over the Middle East, countering agents from the other side, neutralizing them. *Those* were the days."

"In other words, you and your gang of cowboys were killing Soviet agents."

"We were defending our country, pal, and on the best possible battlefield—somebody else's real estate." Cates frowned. "And after we won the Cold War, do you know what they wanted to do with us? Bring us back to the States to tackle gang crimes. We're an elite unit, and they expect us to play cops and robbers in the slums." His face showed obvious disgust.

"So, to keep your glamorous international spy life-style, you got into this technology smuggling scam," Joe cut in. "How does giving secrets to our enemies square with defending our country?"

"We can't let the government completely disarm us," Cates said. "There have to be agents in place, ready to meet trouble."

Tom shook his head. "And if there isn't any trouble, you'll invent some."

Cates's free hand caressed his pistol. "You three have a real problem," he said. "You seem to think you've got command of the situation. But *I'm* the one with the gun. And I have standing orders to waste you three."

"*You* don't seem to understand that this

isn't a quiet little back-alley matter anymore,'' Frank retorted. ''We've reported to our contact at the Network. He's got all the facts we've discovered about your superiors and Laidlaw. And he's got your name, Cates.''

''Yeah—for as long as he lives.'' From the negligent way Cates spoke, Joe suspected the rogue agent didn't think that would be a long time. ''Don't expect your Mr. Gray to come leading the cavalry any time soon.''

Joe and Frank stared at him.

''Look,'' Cates said, in the voice of a busy person who doesn't like to explain things to idiots. ''We tapped the guy's phone. My superiors here and in Washington know what you told him. And they know he doesn't have enough to accuse anybody of anything. He'll have to dig. And before he digs deep enough, our people there will have taken care of him.''

Now Joe and Frank both shot each other sick looks. Their call for help had condemned the Gray Man to death!

Cates smiled, watching the thought sink into his captives' heads. ''Fact is,'' he drawled, ''you won't have all that long to worry about it. We still have unfinished business to settle from that research station, and this time you don't have a van full of tricks to help you.''

Joe and Frank sat very still in their seats. From the corner of his eye, Joe saw Tom try to copy them. He did his best to sit still, resting his hands on Orb. Tom had been carrying the round silvery robot brain when they'd been captured. Now it lay in his lap. Joe felt sorry for Tom, watching his fingers quiver and nervously tap against Orb's silvery metal skin.

Joe swallowed hard. Right now he felt pretty nervous, too. They were stuck in seats, and Cates had a gun on them. Trying to jump him would be suicidal. The man was fast. He could probably put a bullet in each of them before they got close enough to attack. And he was big enough to be dangerous in a hand-to-hand struggle.

If they had a distraction—if Tom threw Orb at the government hit man—maybe they'd have some small chance. But how could Joe communicate that idea to Tom?

Then Cates was talking again. "This is a nice little gun here. Built-in noise suppressor, so it doesn't shoot very loud. Another toy from Laidlaw. Between its silencer and the soundproofing of this van, I could shoot you all here and now. Then it would just be a question of finding a good place in the mountains to dump your bodies."

Joe did his best to hold his voice steady. "Of course, then you'd have the trouble of cleaning our blood off the nice carpet in here," he said.

Cates gave him a brutal scowl for a second. Then his handsome face cracked a smile—a very evil smile. "Some things are less trouble than they seem," he said. "Especially weighed against the pleasure of shutting up your smart mouth forever."

The rogue agent aimed his gun straight at Joe now. His smile broadened as Joe's muscles went taut.

"Jump, boy," Cates taunted. "I'll still blow you away before you get to your feet."

The next thing Joe expected was a bullet in the brain.

The last thing he expected was for the mobile HQ to pitch suddenly on its side.

15

Jack Cates's gun spat steel-jacketed death. One shot, barely loud enough to qualify as a cough. The bullet passed close enough for Joe Hardy to feel the wind of its passage as he tumbled. If the van hadn't suddenly moved, he'd have been dead.

Cates had been flung from his chair, and Frank Hardy also went flying, tossed by the momentum of the toppling van.

Tom Swift moved with the trailer's sudden lurching. He gripped the back of his chair, swinging lightly as the headquarters van thumped sickeningly on its side.

Cates landed on the rear wall of the trailer flat on his back, his pistol still in his hand.

But the gun was way off target. Before the rogue agent could aim again, Tom dropped beside him, kicking the automatic away.

With a roar, Cates surged up, only to have Tom's foot crash into his chest. Bit of a surprise, huh, taking that from somebody you probably dismissed as a techno-nerd, Tom thought. But this nerd is a trained kick-boxer. Cates's eyes were wide with surprise as he headed for the ground again. Then Tom nailed him, clipping Cates's jaw with his heel. While the Hardys were still recovering from their tumble, the fight was finished.

"What happened?" Joe asked, rubbing an arm. "Was that an earthquake?"

"More to the point," Frank asked, "why weren't you tossed around, Swift?" His eyes narrowed. "It wasn't a surprise for you, was it?"

"No, since I arranged it," Tom said with a grin. "While Cates was playing with us, I was tapping on Orb."

"I noticed that," Joe said. "Thought you were getting a little nervous there."

Tom shook his head. "Morse code," he explained. "I got Orb to call for reinforcements—the metal cavalry in the back of the mobile lab."

He glanced at the trailer's exit, which was

now in the ceiling. "Any idea of how we're going to get out through that?"

Tom discovered that Frank and Joe had a well-practiced answer. They joined their hands as stirrups and boosted him up so he could fling the door open. They tossed Orb to Tom after he'd climbed out, then Frank gave Joe a leg up. Finally, the two on the roof caught Frank's arms as he leapt for the opening.

From their vantage point atop the van, they could see Cates's technicians running around the parking lot, shouting, shooting, acting like a disorganized mob instead of trained agents. They were trying to protect their bikes from Rob, who towered in their midst. The big, shining robot had one of the Laidlaw superbikes raised up in his arms. He hurled it, sending the technicians scattering. It crashed into the other bikes, sending them to the pavement.

One of Cates's men brought up his pistol. He fired several shots at Rob, which only *spang*ed off the robot's metal chest.

"I guess we should be glad Laidlaw didn't give them armor-piercing bullets," Joe said.

Rob picked up another one of the bikes, skimming it across the pavement and knocking his attacker off his feet.

The boys vaulted down off the overturned trailer and dashed across the lot to where the mobile lab was parked. "Keep them occupied, Rob!" Tom ordered.

He unlocked the rear of the van, and Frank and Joe jumped in. Then Tom went round to the driver's side door, digging the key out of his pocket.

"Tom!" Rob's voice rang across the lot.

Tom turned to find one of the technicians aiming a heavy pistol at him. Rob was too far away from the guy to stop him. The agent was grinning as he drew a bead.

Then the man's expression changed to astonishment as he executed a complete somersault. Down by his feet, a metal box skittered away on whippy, cablelike legs, one of which Brother Box had used to flip the gunman.

Tom opened the door, then started the mobile lab's engine. "Come on, Rob!" he yelled. "Orb! Call Brother Box in!"

Rob came pounding across the parking lot, with Brother Box skittering right behind him. The whole van shook as they climbed aboard. As Frank Hardy slammed the doors shut, Tom hit the gas, backing out of the parking space with tires screaming.

Half of Cates's technicians were flat on the ground. The others were too disorganized even to shoot at them as they roared off, despite yelled orders from the top of the overturned command van.

"Sounds like Cates woke up from his little nap," Joe said, grinning.

"Well, he'll have trouble organizing any sort of posse to chase us," Rob said. "Their trailer is useless, and after I finished tossing them around, he'll be lucky if two of those bikes work."

"While they're busy figuring out which two, I'll try to put some distance between us and them," Tom said.

"As much distance as possible," Frank told him. "Cates sounded rather upset back there."

"Yeah," Joe agreed. "He was using some words from Mina's vocabulary."

"That brings us to our next problem." Tom sighed as he drove, picking the fastest route out of town.

"As in, what do we do next?" Joe said.

"That's what we were discussing before Cates and his boy scouts dropped in on us," Frank agreed. "And I was about to suggest that we do whatever it takes to find Mina."

"I was thinking the same thing," Tom said.

"Maybe we've got one other thing to do first," Joe cut in. Tom noticed that the younger Hardy had lost his grin. "We have to call Washington and warn the Gray Man."

"They'll trace us again," Tom warned.

"Not if we keep it very short," Frank said. "Frank's right. We owe the man a warning."

"Yeah. He's a friend, kind of," Joe added.

They stopped at the first pay phone. Frank fed in change and punched the Washington number. Several moments later he returned, stone-faced. "No answer," he reported. "Not even a message machine."

Joe's frown deepened. "This is bad news."

"Not just for your friend, but for us," Tom said, starting off down the road again. "We're going to be bucking Laidlaw and his friends alone."

"All the more reason to find Mina," Frank argued. "If you get that hyperradio working, we can get help from her people."

"Yeah," Joe said. "Laidlaw can't reach *that* far."

"We're talking a bit long-range, both in distance and time," Tom said. "And we have no idea where Laidlaw is keeping Mina."

"San Diego," Joe suggested promptly. "That's where they took the wrecked saucer."

"The problem is, San Diego's a pretty big town," Frank said. "I'd hate to go door-to-door, asking, 'Excuse me, have you seen a golden-skinned girl with green bug-eyes lately?'"

Tom frowned, his thumbs tapping against the steering wheel as he drove. A thought was niggling at the back of his mind—something about Mina's alienness . . .

Then it came. "We might be able to pin down her location a bit better than that," Tom said. "Remember what's inside of Brother Box?"

"What?" Joe said.

"Nerves—brain tissue," Frank said.

"Cloned brain tissue from Mina's own brain," Tom recalled with a nod. "Which she communicates with, thanks to those pretty blond aerials that pass for hair."

"So it's just a question of range." Frank's voice became hopeful.

"Orb," Tom called to the round computer, now stowed in the rear of the van. "Ask Brother Box if he can contact Mina."

"It says no, Tom," Orb responded a few seconds later. "They're too far apart for communication."

Disappointment shot through Tom. It had seemed like a good idea. . . .

Then another thought hit him. Computers are very literal. They wouldn't take a next step until ordered to do it. "Okay, Brother Box can't contact Mina. But can he locate her? That's a simpler job."

A second later, the answer came. "Brother Box thinks that may be possible if it gets some help on local referents."

Joe asked, "And what are these local referents?"

"I think we can find what we need in the glove compartment," Tom said. "Road maps."

Frank Hardy quickly gathered up the maps, handing them to Joe in the rear of the van. The younger Hardy spread out the maps in front of Rob. The robot scanned the images with his photocell "eyes." Then he transmitted the data to Orb, who passed it on to Brother Box, along with translations of distances.

In moments they had scanned in all of southern California.

"This is not the data Brother Box requires," Orb said.

"Want to put that in English?" Joe asked.

"That map doesn't correspond to where Mina is," Rob translated.

"But San Diego is right at the bottom of this map," Joe protested.

"Which may mean she's not in San Diego," Tom said. "Keep reading the maps."

Mina wasn't in northern California, either. Tom pulled into an all-night gas station and asked for all the road maps they had. Then, parking at a marked rest stop so they knew exactly where they were, they all fed data to the boxlike alien computer.

"Brother Box says it now has stored the necessary referents," Orb announced.

Tom pointed to a multipen computer plotter

fixed to the mobile lab's workbench. "Can it output the location graphically if we hook it up to that?"

The answer was yes. Tom prepared the hookup, a serial interface, one end of which was simply naked wires. Gold filaments unbraided from the pattern on Brother Box's top to wrap around the bare wire ends.

"It will take a moment for Brother Box to get the feel of the plotter," Orb warned.

On the plotter, paper began to move, and the pens twitched jerkily.

"It is ready," Orb announced.

Paper began feeding smoothly through the plotter, and the pens began drawing something at high speed.

In moments, a map had emerged from the printing device. Tom held it up, with Frank and Joe peering over his shoulders. "What's this odd-shaped squiggle?" Tom asked, pointing at the paper.

"That is apparently the T'wikt'l equivalent of 'X marks the spot,' " Orb said.

Joe made a disgusted noise. "So she's in the middle of the Nevada desert? I think there's a mistake here somewhere."

Tom frowned as a teasing half-memory rose in his mind. "Orb," he ordered, "access the Sunshine file. See if any information there connects with this location."

"A testing site," Frank suggested.

"Or a nice, big spot of empty desert to dump a body," Joe said grimly.

"There is a connection," Orb announced after a few seconds. "The location matches that of Solitude—the private estate of Eric Laidlaw."

16

Daybreak was painting the Nevada mountains in shades of red and gold when Joe Hardy woke from his doze. He was in the rear of the Swift Enterprises mobile lab, and his brother, Frank, was behind the wheel.

After a few fancy maneuvers to assure that Cates hadn't caught up to them, they had set off for Nevada in search of Solitude. Tom had insisted that they drive in shifts, to allow themselves a little rest. Now he sprawled in the passenger seat, asleep.

"How long have you been piloting?" Joe asked, stretching.

"A few hours," Frank responded. "I thought it was a good idea to let Tom get some rest.

Besides, we couldn't talk. Someone was snoring too loudly in the back.''

Joe raised his eyebrows, turning to Rob. "I didn't know that robots snored.''

"I don't think he meant me,'' Rob replied.

"You could have woken me up,'' Joe complained. "I would have taken a turn at the wheel.''

"Make yourself useful,'' Frank retorted. "Pick up the map and navigate.''

Joe looked from the map to the countryside around them. "Are we really sure Brother Box steered us right? There doesn't seem to be anything in this neck of the woods—including woods.''

The road they were on wound through a tortured, arid expanse of bare stone. "There's supposed to be a turnoff for a smaller mountain path,'' Frank said. "It will take us higher so we can get a look at the surrounding countryside. Can you spot it on the map?''

Joe looked from the road map to the printed sheet that Brother Box had output. "It should branch off to the left, winding up toward the ridge line,'' he reported.

"We should get a view for miles around once we're up there,'' Frank said.

"Have we asked Brother Box to try giving Mina a call now that we're closer?'' Joe asked.

"We've tried that several times during the journey," Orb answered. "Although Brother Box could locate Mina, it got no response from her."

Joe frowned. That didn't sound like good news. "We'd better get there soon," he said.

"I think we've arrived," Frank said, reaching over to shake his passenger. "Wake up, Tom."

Leaning over the front seats, Joe peered out the windshield of the van. The path had taken them to the top of a long, low plateau, overlooking an arid valley. And in the middle of that . . .

"We *must* have read the map wrong," Joe insisted. "That's a sports arena down there." He scratched his head, looking around at the desolate countryside. "Although I don't know why a town would build a pro dome off in the middle of nowhere."

Tom had dug a pair of ultrascan binoculars out of the glove compartment and was aiming them at the huge structure far below them. "I think this is the place, all right. How about you, Frank?"

Frank Hardy took the compact glasses and tried to refocus them before realizing the lenses did that job themselves. "Maybe it appears to be a domed stadium on the outside, but take a look, Joe."

Now it was Joe's turn to put the ultrascans to his eyes. The structure looked like a domed sports stadium, all right. But where were the parking lots? Then, too, it would be hard to play football or baseball under the dome's huge, transparent canopy. The grounds inside were bright green, filled with bushes, flowers, and trees.

"Hmmm," he said. "First stadium I ever saw built for championship hide-and-seek. Or maybe hunting. I just spotted a deer in there. What *is* this supposed to be? The next step up from those Biosphere domes in Arizona? Or is it a ground-bound Noah's ark? Whoever built this place seems to have stocked it with everything. I see birds flying under there!"

" 'Whoever' is Eric Laidlaw," Tom said quietly. "It's not a sports dome, it's a pleasure dome. This is Solitude—Laidlaw's estate built for ultimate privacy."

"He lives there?" Joe said, putting down the ultrascans. "Where? Or does he just swing from tree to tree like Tarzan?"

"Aim those glasses toward the middle of the dome," Tom said.

Joe followed Tom's instructions and found a dome within a dome, a small geodesic structure half-hidden behind a stand of palm trees.

"That's Laidlaw's house?" Joe said in disbelief. "But that's like living in a pup tent in the middle of a football field. Okay," he amended the analogy, "this place is a lot bigger than your average football field, with no season seats."

"Why do people always refer to size in terms of football fields?" Frank asked.

"It's the only measurement nonscientific types understand," Tom responded with a grin. Then he warned, "Don't underestimate the size of that inner dome, Joe. There's plenty of room inside for a man who lives alone."

"Well, he won't feel lonely for long," Joe said. "We'll be barging in to visit."

Tom knew that entering the dome would not be a simple case of "barging in." He emptied one of the toolboxes stored in the mobile lab. Then he began loading it with various pieces of equipment, including several things Rob had brought along from Swift Enterprises.

Joe continued to scan the dome with the binoculars. "I'll tell you one thing. Laidlaw spent mucho heavy bucks to build his fortress down there."

"Make that plenty of graft," Frank said with a grin. "That place must use enough water to support a good-size town." He gestured to the desert surrounding them. "Water is like gold around here."

"And gold is usually kept in vaults," Tom

said. "We may have problems getting in." He gestured to the devices he was gathering. "That's why we'll take these along."

They got out of the van. Joe insisted on carrying the toolbox, while Tom carried Orb. Frank went ahead to scout a way down, and Rob and Brother Box brought up the rear. Tom spotted the first defense as they headed down the valley wall on foot. "There are video cameras ten feet off the ground, sweeping the terrain," he warned the others.

"That's a problem," Frank said.

Tom disagreed. "It means we have to pick our entrance point from here and concentrate on fooling that camera." Using the ultrascans, Tom searched the bottom edge of the outer dome. "I've spotted some sort of utility tunnel in the middle of the near side," he said, pointing.

"Yeah," Joe said, taking a look. "With a camera right over it."

They had to time their descent in bursts, waiting to move until the camera was turned away. Tom used Orb to help time the cameras and declared that there was a momentary blind spot in each pass. Giving Orb to Rob, Tom turned to Joe and the toolbox. He removed something that looked like a mechanical bug. "We have ten seconds to reach the outside wall and get up to the camera," Tom said. "I'm depending on you and Frank to give me a boost."

Watching the movement of the mechanized camera, Frank counted down. "Now!" he whispered.

The three of them dashed for the wall. Joe and Frank bent, laced their fingers together, and threw Tom's weight upward as he put his foot into their human catapult. He reached up, grabbed the top of the wall, and slapped the bug on the side of the camera. Then he landed lightly in front of the arched entranceway to the tunnel.

"What will that do?" Joe asked, looking up dubiously as the camera pointed its lens at them.

"It took over the camera. Now it will keep transmitting what it saw in the last ten seconds—before it saw us," Tom assured him.

The two robots joined them as Tom diverted the sensor wires of a burglar alarm on the tunnel entrance. Swinging the metal door open, the boys and robots slipped inside. The tunnel led straight ahead, angling down. As the light faded, Tom dug into the toolbox again, coming up with the light-intensifying magnifier goggles.

"It's not that dark," protested Frank, who had worn the things.

"I'm not setting them for the visual spectrum," Tom said. As he led the way, he kept one hand to the frame, switching frequencies. Halfway down, he stopped them.

"Real trouble ahead," Tom reported. He took off the glasses and passed them to the Hardys for a look.

To Joe's naked eye, the arched section of tunnel ahead merely looked dim. But through the goggles, a webwork of brightly shining bars of light blocked the way.

"Ultraviolet lasers," Tom said. "Break one of those light beams, and an alarm goes off." He looked again. "No, worse. I don't think those nozzles in the ceiling are there for air conditioning."

"Poison gas?" Joe asked.

"I don't want to find out. Rob," Tom abruptly ordered, "set your photocells for twelve-twenty angstroms."

"I can see it," the robot said.

"Orb, check if Brother Box can do the same thing."

After a moment, Orb responded. "Brother Box sees it, too."

Tom went to the toolbox and removed what seemed to be coiled lengths of pale wire with lenslike ends. "Optical fiber," he explained. "Rob, you and Brother Box have to slip these over the emitters and receptors for some of those beams. The laser light will follow the fiber and let us bend the beam enough to get through. The lenses are self-stick after you remove the little paper rings.''

Orb passed the instructions along, then the other two robots crept forward and worked together perfectly. Rob's height allowed him to reach the tunnel roof easily, while Brother Box's cable arms handled the lasers at low levels. In moments, they had opened a pathway through the laser array.

Tom led, then Joe followed, worming his way forward on his stomach. He paused for one glance at the threatening gas nozzles overhead.

Two other laser traps, also invisible in normal light, had to be breached before they reached the entrance to the dome-enclosed forest.

"No alarms here," Tom said, a little surprised. They set off along a shaded path, heading for the dome within a dome that was Laidlaw's home. At one point, they had to duck into the underbrush to avoid a passing robot gardener. The tall, cylinder-bodied machine lumbered past with a rake.

Tom was even more surprised to find no security devices at the entrance to the smaller dome. There was just an open archway, not even a door.

"Maybe Laidlaw thought the outer defenses were enough," Joe suggested.

"That doesn't sound like the Eric Laidlaw we've come to know and hate," Frank said.

As they stepped through the geometric archway that led into the dome, Joe felt a buzzing that seemed to go through his whole body.

"A vibratory screen to keep bugs out," Tom said. "No wonder Laidlaw can afford to leave the doors open."

Joe took a deep breath as they entered the dome. The place had a fresh-air, piney smell, the same as the forest surrounding it. No living quarters were in sight. The dome's interior looked like a museum. Joe saw eight-foot-high panels with paintings on them, illuminated by indirect lighting hidden in the roof of the interior dome.

"This stuff is incredible," Tom said, glancing at one painting, a pinkish nude. "That's an original Picasso from his Rose Period."

"I've seen pictures of it," Frank agreed, his eyes narrowing. "In a book on art crime. It was painted in 1907, then stolen in Brisbane, Australia, sixty years later."

Joe had wandered to the center of the dome, where a huge, thirty-foot-wide well led into the ground. "There are three levels below this one," he said. "From what I can make out from here, they're all full of art, too.

There's also a ramp spiraling down. Maybe we should check it out. Laidlaw has to have living quarters somewhere—maybe there are underground tunnels."

Joe realized that neither of the others was paying attention to him. He turned from the railing around the well to find Tom and Frank staring at something hidden behind one of the picture-bearing panels.

Joining them, Joe stopped in his tracks and stared himself. A glowing golden statue floated about a foot off the floor, surrounded by four ten-foot-high black pillars. The statue was dressed in a gold bodysuit, and a black harness crisscrossed from her shoulders to her hips. It was the exact image of Mina. Her pose showed defiance, but her finely molded features were etched with despair.

How could Laidlaw have had this work of art sculpted in the short time the alien girl had been here? Then Joe realized he wasn't looking at a sculpture. Laidlaw had turned Mina into a work of art for his collection.

Tom finally found his voice and confirmed Joe's suspicion. "That halolike glow is the stasis field that protected her. It's just as I found her when the saucer crashed." He frowned. "But how could Laidlaw know that? And how did he learn to use the stasis belt so quickly?"

"We'll just have to get her out of that aura

and ask her," Joe said. "How did you do that when you first found her?"

"I penetrated the field, like this—" Tom moved forward, his hand out to reach into the glowing field.

But as he stepped between two of the black pillars, a hum filled the air. At the top of the ten-foot cylinders, a thin band of red light appeared, pulsing and brilliant.

Then four crimson bolts of energy lashed out at the spot where Tom was standing.

17

The humming from the laser towers gave Tom a split second of warning. He flung himself back as the beams carved sizzling tracks across the stretch of flooring he'd occupied.

"Take cover," Tom yelled, zigzagging away from the black pillars.

His cry was just in time. The pillars stopped targeting him and threw lances of red energy at the others. Joe Hardy dove back as a beam scored the top of the toolbox he was carrying. "Where do we go?" he cried.

"Let's get behind some of these paintings," Frank said. "I bet they won't destroy the art just to get us."

The only problem was that Frank, Joe, Rob,

and Brother Box were much closer to safety than Tom was. They ducked behind panels bearing various works of art, and the laser towers all began aiming beams at Tom again.

He retreated in a wildly veering path, trying to guess where the lasers would hit. Tom was so busy concentrating on the pillars and their flickering bolts, he didn't realize there was a suit of armor blocking his retreat. He crashed into it, knocking the armor over and sending himself sprawling.

A fine example of medieval craftsmanship dented, Tom thought as he scrambled to his feet. Then he realized that the intensity of the laser attack had slackened. The pillars were now targeting pieces of strewn armor as well as Tom. He watched as a beam ricocheted, reflected by the shiny helmet.

Still retreating, Tom finally managed to hurl himself behind the panel where Frank Hardy was hiding. Risking a stray blast, Frank peered around the panel.

"They're still firing but at the armor," he said. "What's going on?"

"Those pillars must have low-grade computer brains," Tom said. "Once they're activated, they have a map of how this gallery is supposed to look. Anything not on the map gets shot at."

"Like intruders," Joe said from his hiding place.

"Or knocked-over suits of armor." Frank looked worried. "This has to have set off an alarm. How do we get out of here with those things shooting at our backs?"

"We'll just have to try to knock them out," Tom said. "I've got an idea that may do it and let us get to Mina, as well."

"Don't keep us in suspense," Frank said.

"I'll need your help, and it'll be dangerous," Tom said. "All of us will have to step out and see if we can confuse the fire-control computers."

"Great—until one of us gets nailed," Frank said.

"We'll also have to counterattack, but that will be my problem," Tom said. "Ready, guys? Rob? Orb, can you relay to Brother Box?"

"Done," the round robot brain responded.

"Okay. On the count of three. One, two—go!"

Tom burst from cover, throwing himself into a full-body slide toward the wrecked suit of armor. He snatched up the breastplate, a curved mass of steel polished to mirror brilliance. All around him, searing beams of energy flared like a deadly light show, aiming for the others as they darted into the field of fire, then ducked away again.

Frank ran an erratic course, confounding the computer's aim. Joe, moving a bit more slowly, nearly had the edge of the toolbox sliced off by a beam.

Then it was Tom's turn. A blinding beam came straight at him. He held up the armored plate at chest level, and the beam bounced off, reflected in another direction.

Well, it works, Tom thought. Another beam speared at him and was reflected, missing the pillar that had launched the energy bolt by inches. The curve of the armor plate threw his aim off. The metal in his hand was growing hot, too.

A third laser blast came his way. Tom raised the breastplate, turned it slightly, and the beam flew right back to the pillar. A hissing slit appeared in the black skin of the laser tower. Sparks flew, then the pillar went dead. "One down!" Tom yelled.

Joe took out the second, hurling the toolbox at the flashing red slit where the beams were discharged. The heavy box smashed into the sensitive equipment up at the top of the tower, and another laser died in sparks.

Frank dashed forward to interrupt the stasis field and free Mina, while Tom advanced, still holding the uncomfortably hot breastplate. Rob took a station beside him, holding another piece of armor.

But the remaining two towers didn't fire. Instead, the lambent red slits at their tops suddenly went dead.

"Why'd they stop?" Joe asked in surprise.

"I turned them off," a voice said from behind them.

The boys turned to see a tall, well-built older man standing at the top of the ramp that led down the central well of the dome. He wore casual white clothes and sunglasses. His face was movie-star handsome, with a high forehead and slightly thinning blond hair brushed straight back.

Tom recognized the face immediately. This was Eric Laidlaw. Although Tom couldn't see Laidlaw's eyes, he could see the half-smile on the man's lips.

"You know, the newspapers call me the Hermit Millionaire," Laidlaw said in a quiet, almost bored voice.

"I can see why your friends call you Mr. Sunshine, if you wear shades like that indoors." Joe Hardy came forward, almost as if he were stalking Laidlaw. "But if you're alone, all the better. We'll just take our friend and leave."

Tom began to call out a warning. Laidlaw was altogether too calm. If he'd turned off the lasers, he must have something else to defend himself.

But Joe, seeing only a lone villain, made his move. The younger Hardy was good, he was fast. But Eric Laidlaw was faster. One second he was leaning against the railing at the lip of the well. The next he was on his feet, sidestepping, and seemingly just getting off a swat.

Joe Hardy went tumbling across the room, to fetch up beside the open entrance archway.

Brother Box was moving, almost a blur as the square robot rushed forward on its cable legs. Golden wires had risen from its top, and Tom heard the sizzle of high energy.

Laidlaw pivoted, whipping up a short white rod, almost like a penlight flash, which he'd held hidden in his palm. But the thing didn't shed light. It produced a bluish green flash of energy that caught Brother Box right in its front screen. The cubical robot flew backward, almost doing a backflip. It crashed to the ground, inert.

"Rob, get Joe—we're out of here!" Tom yelled. Rob had already moved to see how Joe was doing. Now the big robot picked up the groggy Hardy as if he were a sleepy child.

Frank had used the double distraction to get in range of Laidlaw. He leapt forward, ducking as Laidlaw sent a bolt from the white wand. Frank's bid to disarm the millionaire was lightning fast. He grabbed for the wrist of the hand with the wand. But the wrist wasn't there. It—and the arm it was attached to— smashed into Frank's ribs, sending him sprawling.

Laidlaw made some sort of adjustment to his rod and aimed another energy bolt at Frank as the older Hardy was pushing himself off the floor. Frank was flung back, skidding bonelessly against one of the art panels.

Rob and Joe were past the arched entry of the dome. Tom darted to follow them—no use fighting a battle they were sure to lose. As long as they were free, they had a chance.

But Tom hadn't gone two steps before a heavy steel panel clanged down to block the escape portal.

"Tom Swift, I was impressed by your intelligence when you beat my computer pillars," Eric Laidlaw said. "Don't ruin that impression now."

As he turned to face the man, Tom was all too aware of the strange wand-weapon Laidlaw held. But somehow Tom kept his voice cool as he said, "It won't matter much. Joe will be back with reinforcements—"

Laidlaw laughed. "I should also have asked you not to insult *my* intelligence, either. You obviously have no reinforcements. If you had more force to bring to bear, you'd have done so already."

The munitions magnate shook his head.

"As for your friend going off for help, I shouldn't expect that. The caretaker robots have been programmed to deal with him and that rather large mechanical man you built. If by some miracle young Mr. Hardy gets past the gardeners, he'll still be dead before he reaches the perimeter of the dome."

"I remember the laser sensors and gas nozzles in the maintenance tunnel," Tom said.

"Ah, those were only obvious defenses." Laidlaw suddenly pointed behind Tom. "Why don't you help your friend Frank up? He should be all right by now."

Tom knelt to assist Frank Hardy back to his feet.

Eric Laidlaw stepped up to them. "You succeeded in cracking the best security equipment available at this time on this planet," he said. "Quite an accomplishment—if that were all you were up against."

Laidlaw gave them a small smile as he reached up to his sunglasses. "Unfortunately, it was not. I allowed you in here, but I will not allow Joe and that robot to leave."

He gave them a chilling laugh. "And I have methods that are out of this world."

Laidlaw removed his glasses to gaze at Frank and Tom. The eyes that glinted at them were large, multifaceted, ruby red . . . and alien.

18

Tossing aside the sunglasses, the creature who went by the name of Eric Laidlaw turned his back on Tom and Frank. Neither of them went for him. It wasn't that they were paralyzed by the surprise. Tom realized that they just didn't have a chance against the alien's reflexes and strength.

"You might consider your problems getting in here as a test," Laidlaw said, walking up to Mina's still, floating form. The alien glanced over his shoulder. "An entrance examination."

He stretched out a hand to pierce the stasis field, then caught Mina as she tumbled down.

"Aer'k!" the alien girl cried. Then sentences

in that strange consonants-and-clicks language came tumbling out.

"Aer'k is my true name," the alien male told the boys.

"Sounds close enough to Eric," Tom said, bending to retrieve Orb from where Frank had left the round robot.

Mina whirled at his voice. "Tom! Frank! He got you guys too, huh?"

"He got us," Frank admitted. "For what, we don't know."

"All we know is that he's a lot different from what we thought," Tom said.

"Aer'k is like me," Mina said, "a T'wikt'l. I guess the best translation is 'star-voyager.' We were on the same ship—the one that cracked up beyond Pluto."

"I was chief nucleonics officer." The alien was now unconcernedly removing the makeup that made him look human. "Our stardrive engines went out of phase in the higher dimensions."

"Aer'k!" Mina said sharply.

"Don't worry," the male alien said, his lips twisting. "It's way above them. I ought to know."

He turned back to the boys. "Our vessel was destroyed, and it seems that Mina and I are the only survivors. We were already off course, and our lifeboats were damaged, buffeted by certain effects of the stardrive failure. You can judge how severe that damage was by the fact that both of our ships crashed when they tried to make automated landings."

"What amazes me is how you were able to take over Eric Laidlaw's life," Frank said. "Okay, he's a hermit, but how did you make yourself look like him?"

The alien barked a short, hard laugh. "I look like Eric Laidlaw because I *am* Eric Laidlaw. I was also Eric Laidlaw's father and his grandfather."

Frank Hardy shook his head in disbelief.

"My ship crashed here toward the end of the last century," Laidlaw went on. "Apparently Mina's ship got stuck among the outer planets of this system and took the long route in."

Tom shook his head. A hundred years! Yet the alien figure before him had the look of a person just reaching a vigorous middle age. What things this man must have seen! He could have known Edison, Bell, Marie Curie . . .

"I found myself on an unknown, inhabited planet. First I worked to disguise myself to fit in, then arranged for a way to survive. After that, life has been a case of minding my business, keeping others from taking it over, oh, and aging, of course. It's just a bit more work for the makeup process. And then I had to use younger makeup to turn myself into the son who takes over the business.''

"What about records?" Frank objected.

"The equipment in my ship was up to the job of forging legal papers to pass in nineteenth-century Scotland—that's where I first landed," Laidlaw told them.

"But record-keeping has become more complicated," Tom said, stroking Orb's metal surface.

"Merely more vulnerable to superior technology." Eric Laidlaw dismissed computers as if he were talking of prehistoric cave paintings. "The difficult part was appearing to be in two places at the same time. And even that wasn't so stressful." His lips twisted. "After all, we Laidlaws like our privacy. We're notorious for it. For instance, I live completely alone here in Solitude, just me and the robot caretakers."

Tom had the strangest feeling as the alien spoke. From his tone, Laidlaw obviously despised the humans he'd been trapped among. Yet he seemed almost eager to tell his story. Well, he'd been holding in the secret for a century. Tom stared in bemusement. A hundred years . . .

Laidlaw apparently caught Tom's expression. "It seems that Mina has been excellently discreet. Among galactic races, life spans are considerably longer than on your planet. Not counting her time in stasis, I'd make her out to be—what, Mina? A hundred and ten earth years old?''

''One-thirteen,'' Mina said tonelessly.

There you go, thinking human again, Tom scolded himself silently. Mina looked about eighteen, and that's what you thought she was.

Frank was trying to come to grips with what he'd heard. ''So, first you figured how to fit in on earth and how to live comfortably. Is that all you've concentrated on for a hundred years?''

''There was one other thing,'' Laidlaw admitted. ''Getting off this miserable mudball. It's been my main effort for all the time I've been here. I've worked ceaselessly to spur on human technology—''

He was interrupted by a cry in the T'wikt'l language from Mina.

Laidlaw ignored her. ''I introduced new inventions, but I could see that a stronger impetus was needed. Something to force the humans to innovate on their own. I moved from pure science to political science, manipulating leaders to create a continuous state of war.''

Now Mina, Frank, and Tom all cried out.

Laidlaw simply gave them a proud smile. "The results have been quite remarkable, have they not? I took the humans from steamboats to spaceships in three generations."

Mina was horrified. "Aer'k! You can't have blown off the whole Noninterference Directive?"

Laidlaw shrugged.

"Dat's the basic law of our whole culture!" Mina cried in her Brooklyn accent. "We don't mess around with the politics or technology of other races—especially if they're undeveloped."

Tom's face twitched. So, to these space explorers, humans were just an undeveloped species.

"You try spending a hundred years—your best years—among a bunch of savages!" Laidlaw sneered. "Of course, you were in the xenology section, weren't you? You get along so well with aliens."

"Hey, you're the aliens on this planet," Frank Hardy objected angrily. "There are five billion of us, and only two of you."

"I'm only too aware of the problem of numbers," Laidlaw shot back. "It's been an uphill battle, changing your primitive ways."

"What you've done isn't interference," Mina said quietly. "It's contamination." She made the word sound like an ugly crime.

"Trust you to take the high and mighty attitude," Laidlaw said. "Do you think I'm going to agree to a mindwipe and spending the rest of my life in public service? No, M'na. I still have a hundred and fifty years ahead of me. I'm returning to the homeworlds to live out those years as a wealthy man."

He turned to the two humans in the room. "I thought it would take at least another two generations to bring you even close to my technological needs. But now that I have M'na's ship, I believe I can go home quite soon—with a sizable retirement fund."

Laidlaw gestured to the artwork around them. "There's a thriving black market for backwater-world cultural artifacts on the galactic scene. Although you people are primitive, you're quite talented. And I've acquired some pieces that will sell anywhere."

The alien smiled. "Rebuilding the wreckage of my ship with your technology, I'd have faced some difficult choices. There'd be only so much room, you see. I would have been able to bring back just a small percentage of what I've gathered. After all, I've been collecting the cream of your species' work for the last century. Sometimes it's been difficult. See that object there?"

He pointed to a low pillar that supported a marble sculpture. It was a beautifully carved, not quite human face. *"The Head of a Faun.*

Michelangelo sculpted that when he was only fifteen. The Nazis stole it during World War II, but it was, shall we say, lost during the bombing of Berlin."

Laidlaw shook his head. "Those were the days. War criminals, eager to escape, would part with vast treasures for tiny sums. Do you know I had half the treasures of Monte Cassino from a German general who was down on his luck? For a mistake, that war turned out pretty well."

"Mistake?" Tom repeated.

"When you work from behind the scenes, you don't have absolute control over what happens. Like when I tried to arrange the Third Balkan War at Sarajevo."

"You started World War I instead," Tom said in a quiet voice, his fingers tapping on Orb's metallic outer skin.

"Of course, it certainly got the technological pot boiling. But it had its downside, too. Afterward Hitler and his people got out of hand."

"Yeah," Tom said, thinking how many millions, soldiers and civilians, had died in World War II. "But you got a lot of art bargains."

"And atomic energy established," Laidlaw went on obliviously.

"Of course, that might have made for problems if you goofed and started World War III." Sarcasm was heavy in Frank's voice.

"Not my problem now," Laidlaw said with a shrug. "With what's left of M'na's ship, plus the stored wreckage from mine, all I'll need is some connectors and backups—things even your technology can provide."

"What luck," Frank said.

"In fact, I've even been able to enlarge the ship's storage capacity so I can carry more art." Laidlaw looked especially pleased. "I appreciate that, M'na. When your ship first crashed, I had quite a worrisome time. I was sure you were working on a faster-than-light communicator. That is what you were doing in that old lab, wasn't it? I had the whole contents moved here."

Mina nodded.

"Yes," Laidlaw went on. "During this century, I'm sure the Voyagers established bases in nearby star systems. And if you'd contacted them on hyperradio, that would have meant mindwipe for me."

Mina's face no longer registered shock, disbelief, or anger. Tom read fear on her fine-boned features. "Aer'k," she said carefully, "you've been on this world much longer than I have, and it must have been stressful."

Tom realized her tone of voice was the kind

most people would use when dealing with a dangerous maniac.

"Are you sure all of your plans and calculations are valid?" Mina asked. "I don't see your Brother Box."

"Destroyed in the crash," Eric Laidlaw said shortly.

"Then you haven't been able to look at this with a whole—"

"What?" Laidlaw demanded. "With a whole mind, you mean? You think there's something wrong with my thinking? I've pulled this planet up from barbarism. I'm going home. And if you're reasonable, you and your pet aliens here can help me."

"I don't think I can do that," Mina said quietly.

"Then maybe there's something wrong with *your* mind!"

The alien masquerading as earth man Eric Laidlaw suddenly whipped up his destructive wand.

Before Tom or Frank could move a muscle, a bolt of greenish blue energy had slammed into Mina.

19

Joe Hardy moved as quietly as he could through one of the wilder forest sections of Eric Laidlaw's pleasure dome.

He already knew that the open areas meant trouble. His escape with Rob hadn't lasted more than two seconds before they'd been attacked by a gardening robot. It had been a clumsy thing, with oddly jointed legs, a cylindrical body, and cablelike arms that had reminded him of Brother Box.

The gardeners didn't have built-in tools. The one that had come at them had carried a pickax. Rob had knocked the robot down, and Joe had gotten the ax. Before leaving, he'd used it to destroy the downed robot's camera eyes.

No sense in telling Laidlaw which way they'd gone.

They reached a small clearing in the woods, and Joe and Rob stopped. As far as they could figure, they weren't being pursued. Now they had to decide what to do.

"I'm afraid we're stuck in here," Joe said grimly. "We know the access tunnels leading outside are booby-trapped, and frankly, I don't have the technical smarts to get past them."

He shook his head. Why had he been the one to escape? What they needed was a super-scientific brain. Frank would have trouble. If only Tom were out here.

But he wasn't. They couldn't escape, and Joe was willing to bet that the only communications gear in Solitude was inside the inner dome—locked behind that heavy steel door that had clanged down behind him.

"I wish we knew what's going down inside," he muttered.

"Oh. We do know that," Rob said. "I've been getting transmissions from Orb."

Joe stared. Apparently Tom's robots were like Frank's computer. They didn't offer any information unless you asked. "Give me a recap," he said.

Rob proceeded to tell of Eric Laidlaw's alien origins, about his crimes, and about how

he intended to use Mina's wrecked spacecraft.
"He's just fired a stun-bolt at Mina," Rob
ended, "and is threatening her to force Tom
and Frank to work for him. When she comes
around, he'll use them as hostages to ensure
her good behavior."

"So they're alive, and we've got a communications line inside the enemy's fortress." Joe
shifted the pickax on his shoulder. "We'll stay
put for now, but we'll be going back in."

Tom helped Mina to her feet when she re-
gained consciousness. Her face was pale, but
she braced herself defiantly before Laidlaw's
wand.

"Before you make a splendid speech, let
me remind you that you have two—what?
Friends? Pets?" He tapped the rod in his
hand. "And I can command much more unpleasant energies quite destructive to earth-
born flesh and bones."

Realizing that she was beaten, Mina lowered her head and agreed to help her alien
enemy.

Laidlaw had taken them on a brief tour of
his stronghold. Besides the three levels of art
that Joe had seen, there were two more underground tiers beneath the inner dome. The
fourth floor was a huge enclosed space, an

underground hangar for rebuilding the wrecked spacecraft.

Tom saw the century-old equipment rescued from Aer'k's original wreck there, along with the wreckage of Mina's craft, shipped from San Diego.

The salvaged shell of Mina's saucer craft had been patched with the best materials Laidlaw Industries could provide. Some sections were made of shiny silvery alien metal, while others showed the duller tone of some earthly alloy. The getaway craft lacked the clean lines of the spacecraft Tom had seen. It was still thirty feet wide but looked clumsier, now almost twenty feet high with the extra cargo space for Laidlaw's art collection.

Beneath the mottled patchwork skin, Eric Laidlaw had installed the engines from both ships. He was also working to replace and calibrate various control systems recovered from the craft.

"That will be your job," he told Tom and Frank. "I still have considerable work to devote to the engines. Installing both matter/antimatter power plants has doubled the energy output. I believe the in-system drive checks out perfectly. Now all I have to do is recalibrate and boost the stardrive. . . ."

With that, they plunged into days of punishing labor that passed in a blur. Robots performed the heavy lifting, but all the thinking and planning had to be done by the prisoners—subject to the whims of their alien captor.

On the first day, as they installed some organic computer controls, Mina shook her head. "I'm afraid he's really lost it," she whispered to Tom. "It must be the air on this planet. I don't think it agrees with the T'wikt'l."

At first Tom thought she was making a joke, but Mina's face was dead serious. "Remember back in the mountain lab when Frank and Joe first appeared, and I nearly decked them? That wasn't like me at all. Maybe it's some of those poison chemicals floating in your atmosphere. They may tend to make my race nuts."

If Mina's theory turned out to be true, Tom thought, it would be grimly ironic. Most of the pollution in the atmosphere would be directly due to the forced progress Eric Laidlaw had brought to this planet. He'd created the chemicals that had driven him mad.

"Why do you think—" Tom began, but Mina's hand on his elbow shut him up. Laidlaw's overseer robot was coming over to spy on them.

The robot had the same cube-shaped body and whiplike legs as Brother Box, but there was a long, welded seam around the robot's body. Its interior was very different, Laidlaw had told them. Computer chips had replaced the cloned brain tissues, which had suffered fatal injury during its master's crash. That meant Brother Boss, as they called the overseer robot, was much stupider than Mina's machine. But it was quick to punish nonworkers with a fat electric spark.

Tom and Mina went diligently and silently to work. Brother Boss went over to check on Frank, who was wiring computer circuits into the control panels.

"You don't think Laidlaw's plan is going to work?" Tom whispered.

"I'm no expert in robobiotics," Mina answered. "But look at it this way. This planet is bad for T'wikt'l brains. These organic computers"—she patted the metal casing of the module they were installing—"are all made of brain cells. Some have been here nearly a hundred years, being fed earth nutrients. They must have deteriorated. *I* wouldn't trust them. Nobody in their right mind would."

"But you've already suggested Laidlaw isn't in his right mind," Tom whispered, shaking his head. "He must want to get off this world very much, if he's willing to risk this patchwork ship."

A day later, Eric Laidlaw seethed as he confronted Mina. "What do you mean, you won't put in the life-support control system?'' He held the white power-wand in his hand.

"It's too far gone," Mina told him. "Half the brain circuits are dead. And we can't replace the module with the one from my ship, because that section was damaged in the crash."

"It's a shame I couldn't save the third ship," Laidlaw muttered.

"There was a third lifeboat?" Tom said.

Laidlaw nodded. "It came down in 1908, some years after I'd arrived, in Tunguska, Siberia. But there was nothing to save. It had a catastrophic drive collapse."

"Tunguska, huh?" Frank glanced over at Tom, who nodded. They both knew the Tunguska "event" had produced a blast that had been felt four hundred miles from the impact site. Scientists had attributed it to a meteor crash, a brush with a tiny black hole, or a collision with antimatter.

Well, that's what fuels these ships, according to Laidlaw. I guess those far-out physicists were right on target, Tom thought.

After another day of argument, Laidlaw finally agreed to using an earthly computer system to run his ship's life-support. That gave Tom access to some equipment he could control. A little hacking behind Brother Boss's back allowed Tom to penetrate the security system for the dome. He managed to step down the search for Joe and Rob by the maintenance robots.

Laidlaw will still see them if he checks, Tom thought, but if Joe keeps his eyes open, he can avoid being caught. Must remember to pass on the word to Rob by way of Orb. Now, if I could only figure a way to get those gates open . . .

The closer the escape ship came to completion, the less time Eric Laidlaw spent running his estate and his business affairs.

Sure, Tom thought, why worry about next month's projects when you'll be leaving them all behind?

Unfortunately, Laidlaw also became increasingly less rational the closer he came to escape.

"I don't need backup controls for that system!" Tom heard the alien shout at Mina. "You'll fill up all my cargo space with your stupid backups!"

Filling the cargo space was almost as important to Laidlaw as finishing the systems. Every day, silent robots marched in to stow and restow precious artworks. If the alien was in a good mood, he'd gloat over a difficult acquisition.

"There," he said, pointing to a robot carrying a golden scepter. "That belonged to King Tut."

Frank nodded. "Stolen from the Cairo museum in 1959."

"And worth every penny I paid for it," Laidlaw said in satisfaction.

The robots were moving a series of tall, narrow crates into the cargo area. Laidlaw ordered one of the boxes opened. Inside, Frank and Joe found a carved panel of golden amber, backed with silver foil and decorated with gold and jewels.

"It's from the Amber Room, in the summer palace of the czar of Russia," Laidlaw said. "Almost two hundred square feet of decoration like this. The Nazis seized it during the war, and I got it for a song."

Tom watched even Frank Hardy become used to seeing incredible pieces of loot until they saw a robot carrying a painting aboard— a very familiar painting.

"Wait a minute!" Frank burst out. "That's the *Mona Lisa!* I know it's still in the Louvre."

"It wasn't always," Laidlaw said silkily.

"That's right—it was stolen in 1911," Frank admitted.

"My first great acquisition," Laidlaw said.

"I paid very high for it—but I paid even more to commission the forgery that was returned."

Laidlaw kept driving them harder as the job neared completion, until by the fifth day they were working around the clock. At last the alien seemed to relent, allowing his captive workers to get some sleep. They were escorted to a large common room on the lowest level of the underground mansion, below the saucer's hangar.

Tom and Frank had been like zombies for hours, and even Mina was exhausted. Tom was so tired, he didn't even take off his shoes as he collapsed on a couch in the common room.

They were awakened by Eric Laidlaw's triumphant voice shouting to them. He had his wand-weapon in one hand while the other held the Michelangelo-sculpted head. "The ship is finished," he announced, "and the cargo is all loaded. I had to leave behind some pieces, but not valuable ones."

"So, you're going home," Tom said.

Laidlaw paid no attention. His glittering ruby eyes were on Mina. "I'd take you with me, my dear, but the ship is a bit cramped. Anyway, once we got back to galactic culture, you'd turn me in, wouldn't you? Can't have that. Better to leave you here."

"You're just going to strand her?" Frank demanded.

"Oh, no," Laidlaw said reasonably. "Left alone, she might still build a hyperradio and inform the authorities. You'll all have to die, of course."

The three of them leapt up to rush Laidlaw. But they hadn't gone three steps before they were flung back by an invisible barrier.

"Force field!" Mina cried.

"Yes, I thought that would be the easiest way to contain you all," Laidlaw said. "The system drives on these ships emit fatal radiation. You'll remain directly below the ship, right in the killing field."

He smiled, glancing at his watch. "I just thought you'd like to prepare yourselves for death. Lift-off is in five minutes."

20

I'm getting pretty sick of nuts and berries for every meal," Joe Hardy grumbled. He wasn't starving in the domed forest, thanks to a survival course he and Frank had once taken, but survival didn't mean comfort. It had been nearly a week since Joe had eaten a cooked meal. He had managed to catch fish in some of the ponds scattered around the dome. He hadn't dared to light a fire, though, and he just hated sushi.

Finishing the last of his breakfast, Joe headed for one of the ponds for a drink of water.

"Joe," Rob suddenly said, "Orb's sending a message from Tom."

"Problems?" Joe asked.

"You have to get into the dome now. In five minutes all of the prisoners will be dead."

Joe snatched up the pickax he'd taken from the wrecked gardening robot and quickly took off through the trees. "Have you received the access code for the front door?"

"No, Joe. Orb couldn't score that information."

"Then we either bluff or break our way in." Joe hefted the digging tool. "I guess we see if this can cut into a geodesic dome," he muttered unhappily.

But as they came through the gardens, they found they didn't need a door at all. The ground shook, and the dome above his head began retracting, opening the gardens inside to the desert sky. Ahead, the inner dome was splitting open like a clamshell. But the art gallery Joe remembered on the first floor was gone—the whole place was stripped bare. Where the well leading into the ground had been, a huge elevator platform was rising, bearing up a clunky-looking patchwork flying saucer.

"Looks like bad special effects," Joe murmured. "Well, we can get into the dome. Where do we have to go?"

"Down," Rob said. "There's a fifth level to this complex. I can lead the way."

"Okay. There's the ramp to the bottom," Joe said. "Let's hope that Eric the Alien isn't looking out the cockpit window right now."

Together, they burst into the dome and sprinted toward the saucer-shaped craft. A low, almost chugging hum filled the air. Guess he's going through the countdown, Joe thought. Good. Maybe he really won't notice us.

The only way down to the lower levels was the spiral ramp that hugged the edge of the well. Joe and Rob hit it at a run. Under the saucer now, Joe felt the hum as a vibration that reverberated in his chest, something he could feel in his bones. The three levels they passed had all been stripped of artwork, except for a few pieces scattered here and there.

They reached the end of the ramp at the third level, and Rob led the way down a long corridor to a set of stairs. Joe noticed a set of double doors off to the side, one of them ajar. He peeked in, to find what looked like a regiment of cylindrical maintenance robots, all apparently deactivated.

One less line of defense to worry about, Joe thought.

They reached the bottom level of the dome complex, and Rob set off down another corridor. A door opened, and they saw a square figure rushing toward them.

"Brother Box!" Rob said.

But this robot looked more worn. Then Joe saw telltale signs of welding on what should have been a seamless exterior. "It's a phony!" he shouted.

The boxy robot flung itself at Rob, at the same time sending off a spark that was more like a lightning bolt. The air smelled of ozone, and Joe's hair stood on end.

All Rob said was something that sounded like "Gwarg!" as he went down.

Then the cube-shaped watchdog was turning to Joe, its golden filaments rippling as it prepared to shoot off more energy.

This thing will fry me if it has the chance, Joe thought. Can't let it.

He flung himself low across the floor and rolled toward the menacing machine. When he was within two feet of it, he flung the pickax, and its pointed end smashed though the robot's front screen. The boxy robot shuddered, its cable legs whipping around in a last desperate effort to snare Joe.

He danced aside, bringing the pickax up and down again, bashing at the thing with all his might.

Foul-smelling smoke poured from the robot's innards, and flashing sparks flew into the air. They weren't the same as the box's killer zaps, however. Besides, Joe was now insulated by the pick's wooden handle.

He kicked the dead robot aside and continued down the hall. Time was running out, and he'd lost his guide.

"Joe!"

That was Frank's voice!

The tunnel curved slightly, then dead-ended in a large, barrackslike room. Clustered in the middle of this space were Frank, Tom, and Mina.

"You got out!" Joe rushed toward them, only to smack into something he couldn't see. They had to be right under the saucer, Joe thought. The vibrations actually made his body shudder.

"It's a force field," Mina said. "The projectors are built into the walls over there."

Joe looked where she pointed. A strip of shiny silver metal ran down the middle of the wall, standing out from it slightly. "Where do I shut it off?"

"The controls are probably in Laidlaw's command post," Mina said. "Up one level."

"No time for that," Joe said. He hefted his pickax. "Can I futz it up from here?"

He aimed a blow for the silver strip, but the pick bounced away before it hit. The force field protected its projector as well, he realized.

"Try the wall around it," Mina called.

Joe set to work with the pick, making a hole in the wall. Soon he'd uncovered a large box behind the plaster.

"It's bigger than the usual junction box," Tom called. "Could this be the controls?"

Wrenching the box open, Joe stepped back in involuntary disgust. He'd expected to find wiring and circuits, not a mass of quivering grayish protoplasm.

"It's a robobiotic control!" Mina said in despair. "We'll never trace the circuits in time."

"Maybe there's another way," Joe said grimly, peering into the hole in the wall.

He took off his shirt, wrapped it around his hand, then grabbed one of the power lines exposed by his wall chopping. Tearing the wire free, he stabbed its sparking end into the mass of brain cells controlling the force field.

"If we can't turn it off, maybe we can burn 'em out!"

A sizzle ran through the control node, and the air filled with the smell of burnt meat. Joe released the sparking wire to see the captives burst out of their invisible prison.

"You did it!" Tom said, punching him on the shoulder.

"This way!" Mina called, leading them back up the corridor.

"What happened to Rob?" Tom asked as they passed the deactivated robot.

"He tangled with Brother Box's evil twin over there," Joe pointed to the robot he'd knocked apart.

They had reached the stairs when the low humming that pervaded the air suddenly became higher and higher in pitch. It went from a hum to a whine, then even higher.

Sounds like a dentist's drill, Joe thought dimly, falling to his knees. His hands instinctively clamped over his ears.

"The ship lifted off," Mina said shakily. "At least we were out of the killing field."

"Yeah," Joe said. "But Laidlaw is getting away."

"Let's see how much equipment he left in the command center," Mina said. "Maybe we can track him."

They headed upstairs to the fourth level. Off to one side of the hangar, Eric Laidlaw had a walled-in area—his headquarters. The captives had not been allowed in, so Tom and Frank were as amazed as Joe. Maybe a ring of gleaming consoles with tiny 3-D images floating overhead was old hat for Mina, but to the humans it was incredible.

Tom walked around, noting some gaps in the circular array. But the equipment Laidlaw had left behind represented a treasure trove.

It would be a lifetime's work to decipher and learn to use these computers, which were immeasurable generations ahead of anything human technology could create.

Tom watched as Mina stepped up to one console and began tapping her fingers on what appeared to be a plain section of metal. It must have been some sort of alien keyboard, Tom realized, because the security images suddenly disappeared.

Instead, the air above them was filled with a curving blue and white expanse.

"Looks like a view of the earth from space," Tom said.

A tiny golden thread seemed to rise from the earth's surface, heading into space. Alien ideographs appeared in the air beside it.

"Some sort of readouts," Frank figured out loud. "And is that golden arc the course Laidlaw is taking?"

"Exactly," Mina told him. "According to these figures, he's already above the atmosphere and almost far enough from the planet's main gravitational field to switch over to stardrive."

More figures flashed.

"Any second now," Mina said. "The countdown for stardrive is beginning."

Joe, Frank, and Tom all stared up at the

flickering, unfamiliar figures in the hologram overhead.

"Two, one, now!" Mina said.

The display above them was suddenly lit by an intolerably bright spark—intolerable at least by human standards. Tom and the Hardys flung up hands and arms to protect their eyes. Tom noticed, however, that Mina hadn't moved. She simply stared at the display, which now showed a glowing afterimage, expanding from the end of the plotted course.

For a moment they stood in fascinated silence.

"Is that how your people show the transit into hyperspace?" Tom finally asked.

"No," Mina said quietly. "That's how we show a failed transition."

"Failed?" Frank repeated. "You mean he'll be back?"

"Aer'k won't be back." Mina's voice was carefully controlled as she stood rigidly over the control console. "That was a catastrophic drive failure. The molecules and atoms from the ship, its cargo, and Aer'k, have been dispersed all over the hyperspace continua."

She glanced at the three boys. "Do you understand what I'm saying?"

"I think I do." Tom turned from the glowing, growing cloud on the display to look Mina in the eye. "You warned him, but he didn't listen. Aer'k overloaded the ship. Taking booty instead of backups was a fatal mistake. The ship couldn't make the necessary adjustments.''

Mina nodded. "And it blew up—with him in it.''

21

Mina stepped away from the control console and sank into the seat in front of it. She moved as if she felt every second of a hundred—even two hundred—years old.

"Aer'k was a brilliant engineer." Mina's voice was barely a whisper. "The power and drive setup he designed could have worked. The design and machinery were sound."

"But the controls weren't," Tom said.

That brought a nod from the alien girl—or rather, woman, Tom corrected himself. She was a century old. Perhaps her people would consider her young, given their four-hundred-years-plus life spans. Mina glanced up from where she'd been staring at her clenched hands. She looked very young—and very guilty.

"The robobiotics from my ship were degenerating. The computers from his ship were, well, the only word I can come up with is *rotten*. I ran a few diagnostics and got results that were frightening. It must be the poisons in the air here. They made Aer'k insane, and our organic computers erratic."

"Too erratic to handle the hyperspace transit, especially in a patched-up, barely working, overloaded vessel." Tom's voice was full of compassion. "You tried to tell him that, Mina. He didn't listen."

"I didn't try hard enough," Mina said. "Not half hard enough." She looked at Tom with those unreadable, unblinking alien eyes. "I killed him, Tom. He committed terrible crimes against your planet and my people's law. But to be torn to atoms and thrown all over hyperspace . . ."

Mina shuddered.

"Would it have been better to have him caught and have—what did he call it? Have his mind wiped?" Tom asked.

Her face went masklike. "That's the punishment," she said. "You wouldn't understand these things. You're a . . ."

A what? Tom wondered. A savage? Or just a human?

Mina had never seemed more alien to him.

* * *

Tom went off to see if he could get Rob back on his feet again. The repair job turned out to be minor, less than an hour's work. Tom was running diagnostics on the robot with Orb's help when Joe tracked them down.

"So this is where you're hiding," Joe said, coming down the hallway where he'd fought Brother Boss to the death. "Frank and Mina have dug up that faster-than-light radio you'd all been working on. All the stuff from the research station where you stashed her was jumbled in among his spare supplies."

Sounds like Mina got over her guilt trip, Tom thought.

"Mina's also been talking more about the catastrophic drive failure on Laidlaw's ship," Joe went on. "It sent a huge blast of static across all the faster-than-light communications frequencies. If there are exploration bases nearby—and Mina says Laidlaw thought there were—they'll be sending a ship to investigate."

"So the sooner we get this communicator up and working, the sooner Mina will get away from earth." Tom gave a short nod. "Maybe that's a good idea."

Over the next two days, they ruthlessly scavenged as much alien technology as Eric Laidlaw had left in Solitude. Mina was happy to find Brother Box, although her robot had been stripped of several interface components, including his communication devices.

"It's just as well we can't communicate," Mina said. "I'd be tempted to use him, and I can't trust his computations. Your air pollution has probably glitched his brain seven ways to Sunday."

She frowned. "I can't use him for anything until we've cleaned the poisons out of him." Mina's frown deepened. "We'll have to do the same for my brain, too. I've been fighting some of the weirdest impulses. And I can't help wondering, was this how it went for Aer'k?"

"He had years, decades of exposure," Tom pointed out. "While you've only been here for weeks."

Still, he had to wonder what it would be like to live on a world that was so clean that air pollution could be a fast-acting brain poison. *Does she think of us as dirty barbarians, living in our own filth?* Tom did his best to put that thought aside.

They progressed on the hyperradio, with Tom making a few breakthroughs that rather worried Mina. Now he could see why she'd given them such a hard time on the earlier work. Mina took her people's Noninterference Directive very seriously indeed. She was doing her best to keep galactic science and technology out of earthly hands.

In the end, however, they had a cobbled-together collection of Swift-designed microcircuits and sealed boxes of T'wikt'l robobiotic components spread across what used to be Laidlaw's control center.

"Powering up," Frank reported from his post at one side of the console.

"Nothing's shorting out," Tom said, checking over the circuitry.

"Good luck," Joe said, standing off to one side.

Mina pressed what looked like an old-fashioned telegraph key, apparently a keepsake of Eric Laidlaw. Their makeshift communicator used the miles of above-ground power lines as a huge antenna to fling their broadcast skyward. It wasn't much of a message, just a burst of controlled static across the faster-than-light communications channels.

Tom had calculated that it wouldn't be as large or as deafening as the burst from the hyperdrive catastrophe. But it would be easily detectable by any ships that might come to investigate the original burst.

Tapping the key, Mina sent out a simple sequence of short and long impulses. They had decided that was the simplest message, a kind of universal distress signal, like sending out SOS in the days of radiotelegraph. SOS was a short-long-short signal.

After a moment or two of sending, Mina turned on the receiving equipment. Two of the frequencies she tried were just whistling, howling storms of static.

When she tried the third frequency, the Voyagers' operational frequency as she called it, alien words came through, mixed with the interference.

Tom couldn't make any sense of them, of course—they were in the consonant-click language of the T'wikt'l. But if Mina had been a human girl, she'd have been crying tears of joy.

"They're kind of blown away to be hearing from me," Mina said. "This is a closed planet—forbidden to our explorer ships."

Like a zoo, Tom thought. Don't feed the barbarians.

"The main ship will reach earth orbit in about an hour," Mina said. "They're less than a light-year out. Then they'll send a detection-shielded saucer down to pick me up."

"Just an hour?" Joe said. "Yeesh, when these guys move, they move *fast*."

Mina's last hour on earth was spent carefully rooting out and destroying the leftover star technology. Noninterference to the end, Tom thought ruefully.

"After I'm gone, stay away from the communicator," Mina warned. "We'll be taking it out from orbit."

"How will you do that?" Tom asked.

Mina gave him a mischievous smile. "Oh, we'll just beam down a photon torpedo."

Tom shook his head. Ask a stupid question . . .

The hyperradio receiver came to staticky life. "They've pinpointed the dome from orbit," Mina translated the alien report. "We might as well move outside. The scout ship will be here soon."

They climbed the ramp to the top level of the inner dome, which still lay open. A full moon was just rising as they stepped outside. Without the protection of the outer dome, the vegetation of Solitude's pleasure gardens was already beginning to wilt, its moisture sucked up by the dry desert air.

Tom looked skyward, and a faint throbbing came to his ears. But this was the clatter of a human vehicle coming in for a landing—a helicopter.

"Here comes trouble," Joe said grimly. "We disengage the security systems, and a chopper comes flying down at us. Too bad you already got rid of that stun-wand, Mina."

The group walked out of Solitude and over to the flat, grassy spot where the helicopter was landing. Its appearance had surprised them, just when they thought their troubles were at an end.

But the real surprise came when the copter landed on the lawn and the pilot emerged. He was dressed in dusty outdoor clothes, vaguely gray. His face was ordinary to the point of forgettability. He was the crack agent of the Network.

"Mr. Gray, I presume?" Joe Hardy said as he left the group, walked over to the man, and stuck out his hand.

"Trust you to get here ahead of me," the Gray Man complained as he shook Joe's hand. "Have you got everything under control, or do you need some backup? I have troops over on that ridge, but I decided to come in alone to see if Laidlaw wanted to surrender. The lid has blown off his whole technology smuggling scam. Several bigwigs in Espionage Resources have been nailed, and a couple of Pentagon boys, too."

"Well, I'm glad to see you weren't killed," Frank Hardy said, shaking the agent's hand. "U.S.E.R. had a hit team after you. I tried to warn you, but no one answered your phone."

"After that eye-opening conversation we had, you should have taken that as a given," the Gray Man responded. "You see, I became aware my phone was being tapped right after I sent you to California. I did a little counter-electronics digging and discovered the tap came from Espionage Resources.

"Instead of being a sitting duck, I got the guys who came to get me. They were U.S.E.R. agents, and the whole plot began to unravel. We got their people in Washington, Laidlaw's government connections out here, and the group of rogue agents led by Jack Cates."

"You arrested them?" Frank said.

"Not all of them. Cates was crazy enough to try pulling a gun on me."

"Just as well," Joe said. "He hated the idea of dealing with gangs, and that's all he'd have found in prison."

"Anyway, that's my end of the operation," the Gray Man said. "Now I'm here to nab the kingpin. Do you have Laidlaw?"

"Ah, no," Frank Hardy admitted. "But he didn't get away, either. This is going to be a tough one to explain. First, let me introduce Tom Swift, who helped us on this investigation. And this is Mina. I hope when you see her, you'll believe the rest of what we're about to tell you."

The government man listened openmouthed as Frank ran over the true story of Eric Laidlaw.

"So he was an *alien?* He tried to escape in a flying saucer and blew himself up—is that it?" the Gray Man finally said.

"In a nutshell," Tom agreed.

"I wouldn't believe it for a second if it weren't for the young lady over there."

"Not so young," Joe said. "She's more than twice your age."

"She's also very real and not done up for Halloween. Aliens." The Gray Man shook his head.

"She'll be gone soon," Tom said. "A rescue craft is coming to pick her up in minutes."

The Gray Man's headshake became much more definite. "I'm afraid not," he said. "Young lady—Mina," he amended. "Your appearance here is a matter of national, no, global importance. My government will want to meet with you."

The government man's hand went to the web holster at his side. "Which means that I'll have to take you into custody."

22

Tom stepped forward. "You can't take her!" he exclaimed in horror.

At Tom's sudden movement, the Gray Man whipped a heavy automatic from his holster. He covered Tom with the pistol, forcing him to back off.

Neither Frank nor Joe moved to stop the government man. Mina stood frozen, eyeing the gun muzzle. Tom knew she was inhumanly fast, but could she get in hand-to-hand range before the government man got off a shot?

A sick feeling of defeat drained Tom's soul. This was what he'd been trying to avoid, right from the beginning. Government involvement.

It would be either the freak show or the deep six for Mina. This Gray Man even knew about the rescue ship. What if he decided to try capturing it?

What if he decided to use Mina as a hostage? Would the government try to trade her for advanced alien technology? And what would the response be from Mina's people? The T'wikt'l seemed deadly serious about non-interference. Tom suspected they wouldn't negotiate, nor could they leave Mina in the government's hands.

He turned desperately to the Hardys. "Frank, Joe, you've got to stop this. We can't let Mina be taken prisoner now. Her people will think we're savages."

"That may be," Joe said slowly. "But I'd like to get the straight story out of her, without all this 'I can't tell you because you're a barbarian' nonsense. What if she is an alien spy? I never trusted her, right from the beginning."

Tom stood dumbfounded while the Hardys exchanged dark looks.

Then Frank said, "He's got a point, Tom. All we know about Mina is what she told us. That ship she was on could have been looking for worlds to conquer. The one up there now may have come to finish the job. If we let her go, she'd be able to tell them all about earth's defenses."

"Have you two gone nuts?" Tom shouted. Then he lowered his voice. He had to reason, not rage at them. "Okay. Suppose, just for the sake of argument, a star-traveling race wanted to conquer us. They've got stardrive, robobiotics, and weapons that will make Laidlaw's wand look like a peashooter. What could earth do against that? What kind of defense could we mount?"

"We'd have Mina as a hostage," Joe said smugly.

"If these aliens are conquerors, do you think one hostage is going to hold them back?" Tom demanded. "And if they're what they say they are, a race with a noninterference policy, what happens to Mina then?"

"I think you know," the alien woman said in a dull voice. She slumped, looking even more defeated than when Laidlaw had turned her into a statue.

Tom tried one last time. "Think about it," he begged. "Does anything Mina did during our whole time with her show she was a spy? Or are you going to tell me that Laidlaw was a loyal human who kept her under wraps? Guys, we've got to"—Tom glanced at the gun in the agent's hand—"convince Mr. Gray that this would be a mistake."

"I don't see how we can convince him out of his duty," Frank said solemnly.

"That's right," Joe agreed. "And with this flying saucer coming down pretty soon, I think we should get her out of here. First, let me take off her utility belt."

Joe removed the black harness Mina had been wearing over her gold jumpsuit.

"There's a couple of interesting dinguses on this thing. I just happened to be watching while she operated one."

He turned toward the Gray Man and pressed a stud on the small, boxy apparatus where the straps crossed. With the same movement, he tossed the belt so it draped over the government agent's shoulder.

The Gray Man turned suspiciously. At the last moment, he aimed his gun at Joe, just as a golden glow enveloped him. The agent froze immediately into a statue that might have been titled *Annoyed, Surprised Man with Gun*.

"Sorry to steal your stasis belt like that, Mina," Joe said.

"And we're both sorry for giving you such a hard time, Tom," Frank apologized. "The problem is, there's no way we could argue our government friend here out of what he thought he had to do. I was trying to think of a way to stop him without hurting him."

He grinned at his brother. "That was pretty fast thinking, Joe."

"I'm just glad it worked," Joe said. "That belt won't do him any harm, will it?"

Mina gave them a half-smile. "Oh, he'll probably holler for a bit, once he comes out of stasis. Other than that, no."

"We'll take care of cutting the field and destroying the belt by remote control. And we'll be careful—I promise," Tom said.

Joe glanced at his watch. "I hope this little sideshow hasn't scared off your ride. It should have been here by now."

Tom had a question. "This ship is shielded against radar—I can understand that. But if it's also shielded so it can't be seen, how do you know when it— Whoa!"

A shining saucer, forty feet wide, suddenly materialized overhead.

"The ship becomes visible when you're inside its field," Mina told him sweetly. "And you don't have to worry about being fried by radiation. They've dampened the flow of the exhaust rays that Aer'k planned to kill us with."

"Uh, yeah. That seems pretty obvious—now." Tom and the Hardys all looked up, drinking in the sight of the craft floating like thistledown, feeling the hum of the drive field pervade their bodies. The beautiful, shining craft settled down in the middle of the late Mr. Laidlaw's gardens, right by the still open inner dome.

Tom's breath seemed to stop as a section of the hull slid down, forming a combination opening and landing ramp. An inner seal vanished, and once again he saw the inside of a T'wikt'l spaceship. But this one was alive, bright lights gleaming on the control boards, 3-D holographic images—charts, readings, even an image of his upturned, wondering face—all flashing over the console screens.

Two more aliens of Mina's race stood by the door. Beauty seems to run in the T'wikt'l, Tom thought. He noticed that both held wand-weapons at the ready.

"Yo, guys, looks like it's time for me to take a hike." The tough words in the Brooklyn accent were in sharp contrast to the expression on Mina's face. She was trying to smile, but there was an edge of something else.

"This is a closed planet. I'll never see you again." Now Tom could identify the odd undertone to her smile. It was sadness, a sense of loss.

"You had no need to help me, but you did. I wouldn't be going home without you, but there's nothing I can do to thank you—I'm not allowed. All I can promise is that I'll never forget you earth humans.''

Maybe, Tom thought, just maybe we're not savages to her after all.

"Aer'k accelerated your progress in the sciences," Mina went on. "But most of the hard work you've been doing yourselves. Soon enough, I think, our races will meet again among the stars. I hope I'll be around to see that."

She shook hands with Frank and Joe, then hugged Tom. Bending down, she picked up the inert form of Brother Box with that alien strength so at odds with her slender frame.

Without looking back, she boarded the T'wikt'l scoutship. The crew members were still greeting her as the hatches closed.

Tom, Frank, and Joe backed away from the saucer. The humming became a high whine, not as bad in open country as it had sounded in the enclosed lower level of Solitude. Hands over his ears, Tom looked up as the spaceship rose above them—then vanished.

They were still looking upward, when a sudden hissing accompanied by bright flying sparks brought their attention back to earth—specifically, to the Gray Man.

A bluish light pulsed from the square form of the stasis projector. The black casing cracked, and more sparks flew from the inside. The golden glow surrounding the government agent disappeared, and the belt dropped to the ground. Blue radiance flared blindingly around it for another second. Then all that was left of the device was a scorch mark on the ground.

The Gray Man slewed around, nearly falling flat on his back. "What are you up to?" he demanded, bringing his gun to bear on Joe. "Where did that girl go?"

"Home," Tom said simply.

Frank and Joe explained about stasis. The government agent looked up. He saw no saucer, but his face took on an odd expression. "I noticed that the moon was just past the zenith when I came in for a landing," he said, heading for his helicopter. "It's moved. And so has the clock on the control board."

The Gray Man rejoined them. "And this is what did it?" he said, scuffing at the scorch mark with his boot. "All burned up?"

Frank leaned over to Tom. "Want to bet the same thing happened to the faster-than-light radio?"

Tom grinned wryly, shaking his head. "I'm not losing money on that one. When these creatures don't interfere, they don't interfere to the max."

"Speaking of the max, that's what you three jokers should get, for interfering with a government investigation." The Gray Man's voice was cold and angry. "Maximum penalty. Years in prison. Throw away the key."

Then the agent sighed. "The only problem is, I can't prove anything. Your girlfriend from the stars is gone, and all the alien technology that didn't get blown up in space has already been destroyed."

Tom and the Hardys breathed sighs of relief. "It's really better this way," Frank tried to convince the Gray Man. "Think of the can of worms we'd be opening."

"A story about aliens corrupting government officials is probably the last thing this world needs," the government man agreed. "So what about a more down-to-earth story? How's this: We got onto Laidlaw and his techno-smuggling scam. He tried to escape in an experimental, unproven plane. It blew up in midair."

Tom nodded. It came close enough to the truth.

"The corruption case has enough people falling over themselves to testify and save their miserable hides. We don't need Laidlaw," the Gray Man said. "U.S.E.R. is getting a long overdue cleaning up. If their people are cooperative enough, we may even catch some of the terrorist go-betweens."

The agent looked at the boys. "We'll keep the rest of this to ourselves. Besides, it sounds too much like a bad TV movie."

The Gray Man stepped over to Tom. "I guess the government owes you an apology. I'll do my best to counteract whatever stories the U.S.E.R. gang puts out about you. That goes for you guys as well," he added, nodding to the Hardys. "Maybe we should also give you our thanks. But I'm not so sure of that."

"Hey, if you're willing to forget any charges, I'll forget about any thanks," Tom said cheerfully.

The Hardys came over. "You make a real interesting partner, Swift," Frank said.

"Yeah, full of surprises," Joe added.

"I wouldn't have come through this without you guys," Tom said. "Like the way Joe knocked out that force field."

A strangled sound came from the Gray Man. "Force fields, huh? And we've got no clue how they did that?" He shook his head. "I'd better get out of here before my hair goes gray." The government man turned to the Hardys. "You guys want a lift?"

Joe Hardy grinned. "Why don't we see Tom home first? That way we can explain some stuff to his folks. I think the government owes him a free ride."

Tom shrugged. "Why not? I can have Rob drive the mobile lab back to Central Hills."

The Gray Man stared as the huge, gleaming robot appeared out of the retracted dome, carrying Orb. The spherical robot had overseen repairs to his mobile partner, and Rob returned the favor by once again becoming the electronic brain's legs.

"Just make sure he takes back roads," the agent said. "I don't want any more alien sightings coming out of this."

A week later Tom Swift and Mandy Coster lay on a blanket in the middle of the desert, staring up at the night sky.

"It really is beautiful," Mandy sighed, turning to Tom. "I'm sorry I couldn't make it for the meteor showers."

"There's always next year," Tom told her. "It may not be as impressive, but I'm sure it'll be a good show." He wondered for a second what would have happened if Mandy *had* been along when Mina's ship crash-landed.

Then he pushed the thought aside. He'd almost lost Mandy thanks to this adventure, and that had taught him one thing. She meant more to him than he'd ever admitted to himself. Tom didn't want to lose her again.

"So Frank and Joe Hardy recruited you to help look into this Laidlaw mess we've been reading about in the papers. Then the crooked government agents tried to frame you and silence you." Mandy shook her head. "You took a lot of risks, Tom. Especially with that blond. Where did she fit in?"

Was it his imagination? Or had Mandy's voice gotten sharper there?

"She was a go-between, being used by the crooked agents."

"And what happened to her?" Mandy pressed.

With perfect honesty, Tom was able to answer, "She was sent home."

"Deported, huh? I never believed that Brooklyn accent. She was as phony as a three-dollar bill."

Mandy, you don't know the half of it, Tom thought.

"Well, it's all over now. Your folks must be glad. This whole thing had to be pretty scary for them."

"My father is trying to decide whether to be proud or annoyed at my 'working undercover,' as he puts it. Mom wants me never to do it again. Sandra just thinks it's cool."

"Harlan Ames is very impressed with you—and with that government agent who came to explain things," Mandy said.

The Gray Man had been as good as his word, helping Tom out of any jams caused by his participation in the case. "Hey, you sent us to spy on him," Joe Hardy had said. "The least we can do is give him some slack."

So the agent had pitched in to clear things on the home front. But Tom had decided to try his chances without government aid when it came to Mandy.

It looked like it had worked.

"Well, it's all over now," Mandy said, snuggling closer. "No more dodging bullets or dumping me for my own good."

She put a finger to his lips. "And repeat after me—no more blonds!"

"No more blonds," he promised, chuckling.

Mandy rose up a little, kissed him, then settled back into the circle of Tom's arm.

Silently they looked up at the stars.

So far away, Tom thought. But there is a way to travel among them. I might not be the one to find it, but I know it's possible.

Tom also had some clues—data files that Orb had stored while connected with Brother Box. Of course, they were in an alien alphabet he'd have to decipher. Then to make them work, he might need an organic computer. By Eric Laidlaw's rosiest estimate, those babies were two generations down the pike.

Mandy cuddled closer. Tom smiled at her, then turned to gaze at the stars again. Yes, he thought, he'd keep those files. Maybe his grandchildren would find a use for them.

They'd need them, when they met Mina's race again.